Her British Bard

DARCI BALOGH

KNOWHERE MEDIA

Chapter One

S ofia desperately needed a few minutes to recover after successfully escaping the family barbecue .

Blinded by the glare of the sun, she came around the corner of her father's ancient garden shed and ran her manicured fingers along the outside wall. Rough and bumpy. Flakes of blue paint threatened to come off at her touch. Though the sunlight was bright in her eyes, it did not reflect off the windows of the small building. It couldn't. Years of dust had built up on the glass, leaving them dull and unresponsive to the driving rays of the late spring afternoon.

The smell of freshly cut grass and newly watered flowerbeds pushing yellow and red tulips into the world filled her nose. The spicy scent of herbs growing nearby blended with smoke from her father's outdoor cooker on the patio. She took a deep breath in through her nose then blew it out through pursed lips. Again. Deep, calming breaths.

Normally composed, sometimes to a fault, she had suffered shortness of breath and sharp pains in her chest when well-meaning family members had cornered her by the cake table.

"Are you dating anyone, yet?" Her Tia Maria had asked.

Sofia always hated this question. She shook her head 'no', because she wasn't. She hadn't dated anybody for a long time.

"Now that you're *Dr.* Venegas will you take a look at this rash on my neck?" Tio Francisco joked.

She forced a smile. Everyone in her family knew that she wasn't a medical doctor, but her uncle would not stop with the jokes.

"When will you start working in your office?" Her wide-eyed seven-year old niece, Olivia, asked.

"Shh, Olivia," her mother, Sofia's sister-in-law, Shayna, said. "She doesn't have a job yet." Shayna gave Sofia an apologetic smile. "Although I'm sure she will very soon."

That's when Sofia had started having trouble breathing. Her lungs felt tight, like they were already full of air, forcing her to take shallow, panting breaths.

Henry, her oldest brother's boy, lifted a giant corner piece of her graduation cake from the nearby table and plopped it onto a gold paper plate. The cake was slathered in maroon frosting with gold sprinkles, the colors of the University of Denver where she had graduated with her doctorate earlier in the day.

Being 14, Henry was a little more straight to the point than the others. "How much money are you gonna make when you get a job, Tia?"

"Hey!" Her father pointed at the boy with his barbecue tongs from across the patio. "Don't be rude."

Esteban Venegas, Sofia's father, was a good four inches shorter than his grandson. This did not take anything away from his powerful patriarchal demeanor. He had worked in construction his entire life to take care of his wife and four children and had the build to show for it. Though he had just turned 65, he looked decades younger and he always commanded respect from his children and grandchildren.

Henry slumped a little and looked sheepishly at Sofia. "Sorry, I didn't mean to be rude."

She tried to give her nephew a reassuring smile, but found it next to impossible, because she had started feeling tiny pricks of pain in her chest in addition to the shallow breathing. Was she about to have a heart attack smack dab in the middle of her graduation party?

Under the guise of getting some ice from inside, Sofia escaped her family's good-natured questions and ducked into her parent's house. She drifted to the quietest room, the formal dining room, which had a pair of French doors that looked out over the serene vegetable garden.

In the cool silence of the dining room she put her hand over the pains in her chest. She was too young to have a heart attack. This must be a panic attack. Years of hard work and the successful fulfillment of her own, and her parent's, dreams were now behind her forever. She was Dr. Sofia Venegas with a PhD in Computer Science from a prestigious private university. But she still didn't have a job.

What she did have was a void that she had always filled with academic pursuits. She also had a mountain of student loan debt and a sense of uncertainty about her future that had never before seemed so bleak.

That's when her eyes had fallen on the garden shed.

Sofia unlatched the rickety double doors of the shed and pulled them open with a squeak. The smell of potting soil, dried mud on old tools, and organic fertilizer washed over her. They took her back to all the times she and her friends had pretended this place was a house or a restaurant or a castle.

Walking across the uneven floor the rough wooden planks grabbed at her navy blue stiletto heels. She sat on her father's stool, careful to arrange her matching navy blue graduation dress so no dirt would get on it from the nearby potting table. There was no electricity in the garden shed, because it was almost exclusively used in daylight. That was okay. The meager sunshine that made it through the dirty windows matched her mood. Sofia sat in reminiscent silence, trying not to think about her future.

It wasn't like her to not have a plan. Since she was a young girl she had known she wanted to go to college. That dream had expanded into wanting to be called Dr. Venegas more than anything in the world. This morning that goal had been achieved. Now what?

Sofia suffered from perfectionism. Everything from the way she wore her long, black hair and chose the perfect eyeshadow to complement her green eyes, to her color coordinated outfits and the decor she chose for her apartment, to the way she budgeted her money and kept track of her schedule, all of it was meticulously planned. Even knowing that, she had not been prepared for the rollercoaster of her last semester at school. The coursework, the fear of what would come next, the colossal loan payments she faced, all caused her tremendous stress. Suffering through a panic attack in her father's garden shed she had to admit that while pursuing her dream of becoming a doctor, she had sort of turned into a total basket case.

Over the last year she had tried countless times to write letters of interest to possible employers, apply to open positions, network with colleagues, all to no avail. She always seemed to freeze up at the last moment, overcome with doubt and fear.

"Now what do I do?" she wondered out loud. The empty clay pots and gardening tools on the potting table did not respond.

She sighed.

"Knock, knock," a familiar voice sing-songed just outside the door.

Her cousin, Luna, poked her head around the door

followed quickly by the unmistakable blonde head of their friend, Bridget, the owner of the voice.

"Anyone home?" Bridget continued her bright one-sided conversation.

Sofia cringed a little at being found hiding out in the garden shed. But if she was going to be discovered by anybody, these two were on her short list of preferred friends.

"Hi," Sofia smiled and tried to look composed. It didn't work.

Luna and Bridget stepped into the small, sagging building.

"What are you doing in here?" Luna asked, though Sofia was pretty sure she already knew the answer. She and Luna had hidden here to get away from family gatherings since they were little kids. In elementary school Bridget and their other friends, Angie, Tawnyetta, and Thomas, had joined them more often than not.

"This place hasn't changed one iota," Bridget exclaimed, picking up a dusty mason jar that held half used packets of vegetable seeds.

Sofia and Luna nodded in agreement. Luna pulled two more stools away from the wall and placed them on either side of Sofia before perching on one of them. She wore a flowing light blue dress with fluttery sleeves. The blue complimented her pale brown skin and darker brown hair. She cocked her head at her cousin, concern playing in her eyes.

"You okay?"

Sofia let out a loud sigh as her answer.

"Don't worry, we sent Angie to get drinks...and find Tawnyetta," Bridget told her as she carefully maneuvered her elegant sundress so she could position herself on the other stool and not get dirty. Bridget was a vision in a low cut, pale yellow linen dress. She had picked up a little bit of a tan while on vacation last month and wore it perfectly, as she wore everything.

Sofia smiled gratefully. She wasn't good at asking for help, but her best friends in the world always seemed to be there when she needed them most. As if on cue, Angie appeared in the open door holding two wine bottles. She wore a flower print cotton skirt that fell all the way to her ankles. A light green crocheted tank top went beautifully with it and helped show off her red curly tresses.

"Anyone thirsty?" Tawnyetta's slender frame came into view. The only married woman in the group, she had come back to Colorado from her new home in Scotland specifically to celebrate Sofia's graduation. Married life was treating her well. She looked healthy and happy, wrapped in a tangerine silk kimono style dress that showed off her athletic figure and short, spunky hairdo.

"Where's Mister?" Bridget asked. That was her nickname for the only guy friend in their group, Thomas.

"He's not here yet," Angie informed her. Bridget stuck her bottom lip out in a pout, annoyed at Thomas once again.

"Then he's gonna miss the toast!" Tawnyetta held up six empty wine glasses, three in each hand.

"We brought your Mom's homemade sangria," Angie told Sofia as she placed the two wine bottles on the table. They were still dripping from sitting in ice. A mixture of citrus and red wines, her mother made the deliciously potent sangria then poured it back into wine bottles to chill.

Sofia felt her cell phone vibrate inside her bra where she'd tucked it away before the graduation since she wouldn't have her purse. The other women's cell phones vibrated or rang in quick succession. They all fished their phones out from somewhere in their cleavage.

"Thomas," Luna said. She had been the first to retrieve her phone. "He just got here."

Bridget scoffed. She was always mildly irritated at Thomas when he wasn't exactly in tune with their social activities.

Sofia clicked her manicured nails quickly on the face of her phone and typed in 'garden shed'. He would know where to find them.

Minutes later Thomas arrived with a platter of her mother's tamales. "Your Mom gave me these for us," he explained.

"It's about time," Bridget complained at him.

Thomas wiggled his eyebrows up and down at her. "Hi, Bridge," he said with his most charming smile. He was still wearing the grey suit he'd worn to the graduation ceremony, minus the jacket.

"Where's Michael?" Thomas asked Tawnyetta. He had built up a friendship with her new husband, who happened to be the Lord of his very own castle in Scotland, when they had all met while on vacation there.

"He's learning about the Guatemalan heritage of Sofia's family from her Grandma," Tawnyetta answered with an amused smile.

Soon they were all sipping sangria and digging into the spicy steamed tamales with gusto. As Sofia chewed she looked around at her best friends, all dressed up and squeezed into the garden shed. They had made use of the various benches, barrels and wooden crates for seating and were eating and chatting with the kind of camaraderie that happens only after knowing one another since childhood.

Maybe it was the sangria, maybe it was the calming nature of the garden shed, or maybe it was being with her friends, Sofia didn't know why exactly, but she felt significantly more relaxed than she had earlier. Not totally anxiety free, but better.

"So," Thomas finished chewing and swallowing as he looked at each of them in turn. "Why are we here and not at the party?"

All eyes turned to Sofia whose pulse quickened again. She

was in the middle of taking a drink and almost choked as she swallowed.

Luna took over for her. "Family," she said.

They all nodded knowingly and mumbled their condolences.

"But it's not just that, is it?" Angie asked in that half psychic way Angie sometimes possessed. Her deep brown, almost black, eyes watched Sofia with love.

Sofia shifted uncomfortably on her seat. No words came to her, just a hot lump at the back of her throat that threatened to turn into tears.

"Fifi, are you going to miss being in school?" Bridget guessed at the problem.

Sofia lifted one shoulder and let it drop as she shook her head. "Yes and no," she managed.

"I hope you're proud of yourself," Tawnyetta chimed in. "I know I'm proud of you." She looked at the others for support.

"Yeah, Sofia," Thomas said. "We're all proud of you!"

Luna reached over and threw her arm around her cousin's shoulders. "You're a doctor, girl! That's amazing!"

"I'm a doctor of nothing," Sofia blurted out.

There was a pause, then Thomas said, "I don't think they give those kind of doctorates out."

Sofia laughed, snorted more like it, and they all cracked up. Thomas stood and moved toward her, bending down to give her a sheepish smile and kiss her on top of her head.

Sofia wiped tears of sadness and laughter from her eyes and took a deep breath before admitting, "I don't have a job lined up. I haven't even looked for one...not really."

Her five best friends in the world looked at her, stunned.

"I tried to look for one. I sent out letters...well, some letters." She put her glass heavily down on the potting table. Rubbing her temples with the tips of her fingers she said, "I don't know what I'm going to do."

Her friends exchanged worried glances, but none of them had a great idea to throw in her direction. It helped that they were emotionally supporting her with sympathetic silence, but a great job prospect would also have been nice.

A soft knock on the side of the shed brought her out of her miserable reverie. Her mother, soft and round, peeked around the doorway. Her long, greying hair was swept into a stylish bun and a few loose tendrils of it fell sideways as her head stayed tilted to the side. She smiled at them.

"Hija," she said as she looked at Sofia warmly. "Everything okay?"

Sofia nodded assuredly. "Yes, Mama." Again her friends shared glances, but not so much that her mother could see.

Silvia Venegas stepped into the garden shed, effectively filling the only empty space in the center of the crowded little building. "You're all so grown up," she said, fluttering her hand at her throat as if to wave away any emotion that hovered there.

"Oh, Mama," Sofia went to her and gave her a hug. "We're just taking a break from the party. We'll be back out in a minute."

Her mother waved her hand again, but this time in the air as if shooing a pesky fly. "No, no, no, you have fun with your friends. You deserve it." She stood on her tiptoes and gave Sofia a kiss on the cheek. "But I forgot something," she said as she fished around in the wide pocket of her skirt.

"What is it?" Sofia asked.

Her mother pressed a thick envelope into Sofia's hand. For a moment Sofia was afraid it was money and started to refuse. There was no way she was taking any more money from her parents. She stopped short of speaking when she saw that this envelope had been stamped and mailed and was formally addressed to Miss Sofia Venegas. The return address was the official stationary of King's College in London, England.

"It came yesterday and I forgot to give it to you with all of the excitement." Her mother squeezed Sofia's hand. "It looks important."

As she stared at the envelope the heavy oppressive feeling that had wrapped around Sofia for months shifted into something else–a quivering sensation deep in the pit of her stomach, like when she was about to jump off of a diving board, or throw up.

"What's it for?" Luna asked.

"I don't know," Sofia answered.

"Open it," Bridget suggested. "Maybe it's good news."

Everything around her faded into a blurry background as Sofia slipped her nail under the back flap of the envelope. Her fingers trembled slightly as she pulled a fat packet of papers printed on expensive stationary from the envelope and opened them. A hushed silence hung in the air as she read through the first paragraph once, then twice, to be sure she had read it correctly.

"What is it?" Thomas finally asked for the group, who were all waiting impatiently for what appeared to be big news.

She looked up at them in disbelief. Gripping the letter tightly to make sure she didn't drop it or, worse, allow it to disappear into thin air, she answered, "It's a job offer."

As her friends erupted into congratulations around her, Sofia's nerves peaked again. The letter felt like more than just a job. It felt like a turning point. The problem was, Sofia didn't know what direction it would take her, and if it was the direction she really wanted.

Chapter Two

T he streets of London were cramped and wet. At first, walking down them on her way to her new apartment, or 'flat' as they called it here, reminded Sofia a little of New York, but with shorter buildings and funnier looking cars all driving the wrong direction. By the second day, however, she decided they were more like the streets of Boston, a city that had been built without taking cars and traffic into consideration.

The buildings were old and many were made of stone. Whole blocks were attached with no alley in between, though they were completely separate and unique buildings on the inside. Names of places were familiar to her; Fleet Street, Picadilly, Drury Lane, Waterloo, Trafalgar Square, and London Bridge to name a few. But that's where the familiarity ended. Everything else was absolutely new.

She had rented a one-bedroom flat several blocks away from the campus and without a view of the Thames River. This was an economic choice and satisfied her pragmatic personality. She would not be spending much time in her flat, so there was no need to worry too much about what she would see out her window.

By some miracle of miracles one of the few letters she had sent out during the last semester of school had made it through whatever labyrinth necessary to garner a 'yes' response and she was starting her career as a Research Assistant in the Natural and Mathematical Sciences Department at King's College London. It sounded impressive, because it was. King's was one of the most prestigious institutions in England. And her department was located at the Strand campus in the heart of London.

Sofia had yet to lay eyes on the campus, however. Partly because she wanted to spend her first week in London moving into her flat, and partly because she was too nervous to go there yet. As the newbie at the university, Sofia felt a lot of apprehension about her first day at work. She chose not to step foot anywhere near the place until it was absolutely necessary.

She had found her flat with the help of a kind administrative assistant at the university and some serious online searching. It was a one bedroom, about 600 square feet. The living area had a window overlooking the street on one end and a small kitchenette on the other. Hardwood floors in that room stretched into the tiny bedroom, which she was surprised to find didn't have a closet. Instead there was a small wardrobe, just like she'd seen in movies.

"Charming," she told Luna who was touring the place with her via cell phone on her first day there. "But where will I put my clothes?" She turned her cell camera so Luna could see the wardrobe.

Luna chuckled on the other end of the phone. "That looks like it will barely fit all of your shoes!"

The hardly there bathroom off the bedroom consisted of a toilet, a half-sized sink with what she considered a travel sized mirror hanging above it, and a small shower. When Luna saw the images she wondered out loud how Sofia would do her hair and makeup in this diminutive space.

"I'll manage," Sofia told her. So thankful to have a job, and a place to sleep while she went to her job, Sofia was feeling brave about her new life. She would learn to live with England's apparent love of small spaces.

The flat had come furnished. A faded blue plaid sofa and a drab bookshelf in the living area, a round bistro sized table with two wooden chairs next to the kitchenette, and a double bed, which was barely bigger than a twin size bed back home, wedged into the bedroom, were provided at no extra fee. What the apartment lacked in pizazz it made up for in price, not to mention the fact that it was clean and seemed sturdy and safe. She was located on the second floor of a four-story building. There was no elevator. This would give her better leg muscles, she told herself. There was also no air conditioning. Arriving mid-August, that was the only part of the deal that was worrisome.

Though furnished, the flat did not come with pots and pans or dishes for the kitchenette, nor bedding for the bed, nor rugs for the hardwood floor. Sofia spent several of her first days in London hunting down little shops in the area where she could purchase some of these items. She had no car, which was fine because she did not want the extra stress of trying to learn how to drive on the wrong side of the road. She walked everywhere she went and enjoyed getting to know the city a little. After a few days of wandering and poking her nose into every nearby shop, Sofia found plenty of house warming items to lug back to her building and up two flights of stairs.

She opted for a bright and quirky look to keep her mood up, in case she started feeling too homesick. New yellow curtains replaced the old brown ones, a yellow rug in front of the couch, and a yellow and blue striped throw finished off her living room. For her tiny kitchenette she found a bright blue tablecloth and a yellow vase for the table. She also found darling yellow and white checked dishes at a second hand place. They were on sale because there were only enough place settings for four. Sofia bought them, figuring it was unlikely she could ever fit more than three other people in her flat anyway.

She chose blue and white as the color scheme in her bedroom. She bought a blue and white floral comforter, blue curtains, and two small blue and white rag style rugs. She placed one rug on the side of her bed where she stood when she got up each morning and one on the floor of the tiny bathroom. Then she hung blue and white towels and washcloths in the bathroom. Then she was done. Totally decorated, totally organized, with days and days to spare before she started her job.

On the third day at her new place she was surprised to hear a sharp knock on the door. She opened it to a deliveryman with a huge bouquet of flowers from Lord and Lady MacBrody, or Michael and Tawnyetta as she knew them. The flowers took up every bit of space on her small kitchen table, but they were beautiful. With the flowers came a handwritten note from Tawnyetta.

'So wonderful to know you're on our side of the pond now! We'll be down to visit you as soon as we can get away. Love, Tawnyetta and Michael'

As the days ticked off before her first day of work, the flowers on her table bloomed then started to wither. Still, she enjoyed them each morning. Looking at them made her feel just a little less lonesome. At least she had one friend in the same country where she lived.

Though her flat had no view to speak of, she was just blocks away from the Thames. She took a daily stroll to the river and found the way the sky opened up as she got closer and closer to the water exhilarating. Tall, ornate lamp posts with golden fish statues bigger than her head placed decoratively around the base were on every street corner. The Thames itself was wider and more industrial than she had imagined it would be. Still, it had a tree lined pathway that stretched along the edge. Benches were placed facing the river so she could look out over the water and watch the ships go by. Or the people.

She liked London. She liked her new flat, and the river, and the neighborhood.

"I've fallen in love with tea and biscuits," she told Bridget when she called one afternoon to see how Sofia was fairing.

"Oh, Fifi," Bridget giggled. "You sound so British already!"

One of Sofia's favorite discoveries was a narrow, unassuming bookstore called The Red Lion Bookshop, a sliver of a building nestled between a bank and another office building. Those buildings looked as if they'd been built within the past 50 years, while The Red Lion Bookshop looked as if it had been zapped into the alley between them by an old wizard who wanted to inject a sense of ancient whimsy into the space.

Narrow didn't quite describe this bookshop. Once inside there was just enough room for two people to pass...almost. The shop was crooked, too. The floor sloped to the right at the entrance then slowly rolled underfoot until it was sloping decidedly more to the left at the back of the shop. A tilted staircase led precariously up to a second then a third floor. Despite the obvious violation of modern day building codes, the tight and twisted qualities only added to The Red Lion's charm.

That's where she had gone on the Friday before she was to start her job. She returned happily from The Red Lion with an armful of new and used books to stack on her empty bookshelf. Just as she deposited her purse on the couch and the books in a neat line on the top shelf, there was a knock on her front door.

Sofia glanced at the bouquet of flowers on her kitchen table. It couldn't be another delivery from Tawnyetta. She stepped to the door, pulled it open, and was completely surprised at who she found on the other side.

Chapter Three

"Bea!" Sofia declared.

Bea and her husband, Travis, were standing at her door. Sofia had gotten to know the couple while staying in Scotland at Tawnyetta's castle...before it was Tawnyetta's castle. Short and spunky, and always up for a laugh, Bea had been easy to know and like. Travis, on the other hand, had spent most of the time with his father and brother-in-law and came across much more reserved than his wife.

"Sofia!" Bea threw open her arms.

Sofia leaned down to give her a hug. "Come in," she said as she stepped aside and made room for them to enter. "What are you doing here?" Sofia asked as she motioned for them to take a seat on the sofa.

"You're in London," Bea said as she sat down and patted the seat next to her for Travis to take. She waved her hand back and forth between the two of them and Sofia. "*We're* in London."

"Right, of course," Sofia said. She had included Bea on her list of people to contact in London, but had not had the time to reach out to her just yet.

"Tawnyetta told us your address and we thought we would pop by as a surprise." When Bea said 'pop' she flared her fingers out and wiggled them. Jazz hands.

Sofia smiled. "Would you like something to drink?"

Luckily, she had been to the liquor store the day before and picked up a bottle of white wine. She offered it to them in the yellow and white checked coffee mugs from her cupboard.

"Sorry, no wine glasses yet," she explained.

Bea giggled. Bea was always giggling at something. "These are darling! Aren't they, Travis?"

Travis, a tall, droopy looking man, nodded without looking up. "Tastes the same either way," he said quietly then quickly downed half of the wine in his cup in one gulp.

"How do you like your new place?" Bea asked.

"I like it just fine. Just settling in."

"When do you start at King's?" Bea seemed well informed about Sofia's life. Sofia didn't mind. It was nice to talk to friendly faces.

"Monday morning," she answered as she poured more wine for Travis. He had swallowed the second half just as quickly as the first.

"Travis studied there," Bea offered this information as she nudged her husband.

Travis looked up from his cup and let the comment register before responding, "Oh, yes, yes." It was obvious to Sofia that he had been coached by his wife before they got there. "I did. Fine university. What department will you be in?"

"Natural and Mathematical Sciences."

To her surprise, Travis' droopy eyes lit up. "That was my department."

"Really?"

To say that Travis was an introvert was probably an understatement. Now that he had gulped down a glass of wine and found out that Sofia shared his math and science brain, he loosened up.

"Wait," he said as he sat forward on the cushion. "Will you be working with Professor Shipley?"

Just the mention of the man's name hit Sofia's internal nervous button. She nodded 'yes'.

Travis blew a quiet whistle. "That's a challenge, that is."

"Now, now," Bea nudged Travis again, this time a bit harder than the first time. "We came by to invite you to dinner, not talk about crusty old professors." Travis didn't appear to hear her at first. She nudged again.

"What's that?" he said as he turned to his wife. She raised her eyebrows at him and her meaning came through. "Of course, of course, won't you join us for dinner tomorrow night?" Travis asked Sofia.

Sofia hedged for just a moment before answering, "Thank you, that's very nice. I would love to."

The next evening it was Sofia's turn to knock on a door.

She had found Bea and Travis's small house with not too much trouble. Thank goodness for the taxi service. Their home was in Hampstead, which was a pretty area. A charming stone walkway led to a front door that was painted robin's egg blue. An iron fence flanked both sides of the path. So many flowers and shrubs filled the small front yard that they spilled over the fence and their scent filled the air, bringing lightness to Sofia's heart. She was glad to be settled into her new place and happy to be joining friends for dinner. Everything about her new life here seemed to be coming together. Maybe she could start to relax.

She shifted the bottle of wine she'd brought as a gift into her left hand where she already held her purple sweater, it might rain later in the evening. She knocked on the blue door with her free hand. The muffled sound of talking and laughing came through from the other side. She heard footsteps getting louder as they neared, the click of a lock disengaging, then the door pulled open.

The smile she expected to give Bea froze on her face and her greeting stuck in her throat. It wasn't Bea who answered the door. Nor was it Travis as she might have expected. It was, instead, a complete stranger. A man. Tall, fair-skinned, with deep red hair cut short and styled well. He had a strikingly handsome face that left her searching for words and...was she seeing it right? Yes, she was. Golden yellow eyes.

Sofia opened her mouth then shut it again. She was overcome with the feeling that she'd seen him before...but no...that would be impossible.

"I'm sorry," she stammered as she looked at the numbers over the door for verification of where she was. "I must have the wrong house." Sofia stepped back so she could retreat to the sidewalk and regroup when the man spoke up and stopped her.

"Wait, no, you're Sofia, right?"

She halted and looked more closely at him. "Yes, I am. Do I know you?"

"Not yet," the man smiled and it seemed to light up the space around him. "I'm Ian," he said. Then he stepped back into the door and gestured for her to come inside. Her eyes were drawn to his arms, exposed by his short-sleeved shirt. They were taunt and roped with muscle. They were also covered with tattoos. "Bea and Travis are in the kitchen wrestling with some kind of lamb dish. They asked me to get the door." His voice was deep, smooth, a British accent of course.

Ian. Ian? Where did she know him from?

Sofia came through the door cautiously and went straight

into a tight entryway. Ian pressed himself against the wall with one arm stretched out to hold the door open for her as she came in. The space was so small that they ended up very close together. As Sofia inched carefully by him she took in his excellent bone structure, the golden yellow of his eyes, his cologne–which was completely distracting–and the tattoos on his neck snaking out from under the collar of his shirt.

Tattoos. Tattoos! That's why he looked familiar. She looked up at him with sudden recognition. This was the lead singer of the band at Tawnyetta's wedding. What were they called again?

Ian grinned down at her in a kind of 'I know you but you don't know me' way as she made her way by him. One wrong move by either of them and their bodies would touch in several different places. Her eyes wandered quickly down his lean form and decided that wouldn't necessarily be a bad thing. She remembered the rush of excitement she had felt when he winked at her from the stage at Tawnyetta's wedding reception. The sex appeal he exuded while performing had been enticing.

"Aren't you?" She stopped. She could not remember the name of the band. "Weren't you...?"

Ian lifted his eyebrows waiting for her to finish.

"Didn't you sing at the wedding? At the castle?" She finally got the words out, if a bit awkwardly.

His face so close to hers, already amused, broke into another wide smile that spread so completely across his expression it was like he was shining. Then he ducked his head down in a half proud, half embarrassed way. He lifted his gaze to hers from that position and his smile came from deep in his eyes. Goosebumps shimmered up her arms and across her neck.

"Yes, I did. For Michael, er, I mean Laird MacBrody."

He switched his British accent to Scottish brogue as he said Michael's title with a flourish, making her smile then blush. A reaction to their closeness and his intensity. Was it getting hot in here? She suddenly realized that she had not yet moved all the way past him and their bodies were still in danger of pressing against each other. She stepped further down the hallway, her heels clicking on the tiled floor.

Sofia had dressed semi-casual for the evening. She wore crisp tailored grey slacks that cropped just above her ankle and had topped them off with a baby doll style, black blouse that showed off her bust line. Her heels were a cute pair of sling back sandals. Her straight, black hair was up in a knotted bun, but long tresses in the front fell down and framed her face. She called it her 'Meghan before she married Harry' bun.

Ian had on a pair of dark jeans and a black short-sleeved button up shirt. Though monotone, the shirt had a sleek, sexy, rockabilly look to it that definitely gave him a musician vibe. Or maybe it was the tattoos. Sofia was still in the middle of the small hallway looking back at him, and he at her, when Bea called out to her from somewhere deeper in the house.

"You remember Ian, don't you Sofia?"

Sofia broke the look she was sharing with Ian and turned to Bea, but not before she saw a sparkle in Ian's strange, gold eyes. "Yes," she said to Bea. "From the wedding."

Bea ushered her into a smartly decorated dining area where four places were set at a dinner table and said, "Yes! The Robot Tellers!"

That's right, that was his band's name.

Travis, wearing a full size floral print apron, joined them from the kitchen. His face brightened when he saw her. "Hello, Sofia."

"Hello," Sofia said as she lifted the wine bottle. "I brought some wine for dinner."

Dinner, it turned out, was the four of them; Bea, Travis, Sofia, and Ian. Having an attractive man as the unexpected fourth threw Sofia for a bit of a loop. However, Bea was so good at keeping up the conversation and Travis was much less introverted in his own home, all of which made the whole night tolerable. More than tolerable if she was being honest. The wine helped, too.

Ian was an old college friend of Michael's and hadn't known Bea and Travis before the castle wedding where Sofia had seen him perform. Bea and Travis had stopped to help Ian and his band on the side of the road while driving back to London. Ian's van had broken down. They'd since become friends.

"I still don't know if Ian was more concerned about getting his band mates home or his guitar," Travis said with a chuckle.

"Guitar, absolutely," Ian responded. "And, I guess the drum set, too." He leaned back in his chair, a move that showed off a strong, flat abdomen underneath his sleek shirt. He looked at Sofia, the sparkle he'd had in his eyes when she left him in the hallway was there again. "Do you like music?"

Sofia found it impossible to look away from him. The color of his eyes was strange. She'd never seen anything like it. Tawnyetta had amber eyes that could glow a liquid golden brown, which were quite arresting. But Ian's eyes were golden yellow all the time. Like a cat. They flashed with intelligence, humor, and something Sofia couldn't quite put her finger on, something electrifying.

"Um, yes, I like music," she stammered.

Seated across from her, Ian leaned forward and put his elbows on the table, his colorful tattoos in stark contrast to his pale skin. He continued to hold her gaze with his. "Who do you like?"

Sofia could not think of one band that she could mention. Not one singer or musician came to mind. She had always been terrible at remembering names of bands or the songs they sang. With Ian watching her it was impossible for her to answer. She drew a complete blank.

A beeping noise erupted from the kitchen.

"The meat pie!" Bea exclaimed. She and Travis both hopped up from the table and rushed into the kitchen, the bow on the back of Travis' apron flopping wildly as they disappeared through the door.

"Lamb pie," Ian said.

Sofia turned her attention back to him and became intensely aware that they were quite alone in the dining room. "Is that what we're having?" She'd never had a meat pie and wasn't sure it sounded very appetizing. To be polite she said, "It smells good."

"It smells delicious. I don't get many home cooked meals anymore, so it's a real treat."

"Do you travel a lot with your music?" Sofia managed to come up with a semi-intelligent question.

Ian nodded and picked up the open bottle of wine. "May I?" he asked as he tipped it toward her glass, which was almost empty. She nodded. He spoke as he poured, "Yes, I do a lot of takeaway."

Her mind clicked through the possible meanings of that statement. Finally it landed on one that made sense. "Right, takeout. Me too, especially since I got here. I don't have much of a kitchen at my apartm—at my flat."

The sound of lighthearted bickering in the kitchen drifted over the guitar music Bea had put on for ambience. They both paused then shared a smile.

"Married life," Ian said wryly.

Sofia laughed sharp and loud. It was such an unexpected sound she shut her mouth tight to stop it. He grinned at her, his eyes gleaming with that odd intensity again. Embarrassed at her outburst she looked down at her wine glass and took a deep sip, wondering what else they could talk about.

"You should come to a concert," Ian said. He had leaned back in his chair again and was sipping his wine, looking at her over the glass.

"Your concert?"

He nodded and swallowed. "Yeah..." his cat eyes continued gazing at her. Then, as if he'd realized he was staring, he looked down at his hands. His shoulders hunched forward just a bit and she got the distinct impression he had turned shy all of a sudden. "If you want. You may not like it."

A flutter of nerves erupted in her stomach. Was he asking her out? She couldn't tell for sure. The fluttering increased and Sofia took another sip of wine. Washing her nervous stomach with wine didn't do much to reduce her nerves. She didn't know if she would be capable of eating anything called lamb pie.

"I've heard you sing," Sofia said. She meant it as proof that she had enjoyed his performance. That's not how he took it.

"Ouch," he responded.

"No, that's not what I meant," Sofia started to explain.

"Rosemary and garlic lamb pie," Bea announced. She held a bowl of tossed greens while Travis followed her, savory lamb pie in his oven mitt covered hands.

Dinner was on. The time to explain herself to Ian was over. As the meal and conversation progressed Sofia realized it wasn't that important. It's not like she had been looking for a date, especially not with a rock musician. She couldn't deny the attraction between them, but in the real world he wasn't her type. Besides she had bigger concerns looming on the horizon. Monday morning she would be reporting to her first day at work, and when she remembered that fact the fluttering nerves in her stomach morphed into full-blown tremors of anxiety.

Chapter Four

As Sofia made her way from the Victoria Embankment along the River Thames into King's College Strand Campus on Monday morning she felt like Alice in Wonderland.

Outside, along the river where she'd grown comfortable over the past week, she was normal sized. Once she walked under the King's College ancient archway built from smooth, shaped stone with the glowering face of a bearded man she assumed was King George IV hovering over her, Sofia started shrinking.

The buildings were grand and intimidating. They stretched five and six stories high, built from smooth marble and pure white stone, with huge pillars as big around as her first car gracing their fronts. She made her way across the great courtyard, through crowds of students who were either busily moving from point A to point B or relaxing in the sun at outdoor tables, and past the four rows of fountains that shot never ending streams of water straight into the air until they reached the limits of gravity and plummeted back to the flat stone tiles with a great splash. By the time she reached the fountains, Sofia felt only five inches tall.

She paused in the cool mist coming off of the splashing water. She had heard once that anxiety was just a form of excitement, but with the brakes on. On this morning, standing in the middle of this historic place, an academic powerhouse like King's, world renowned, respected, and resplendent, Sofia finally understood that saying. The magnitude of being invited to work with some of the most respected academics in the world lifted her spirits to a thrilling height. The realization that one misstep, one stupid mistake, could bring it all to an end, made any amount of excitement she felt come to a screeching halt.

Her research assistant position was not as permanent as she had led her family and friends to believe. How could it be? She had never interviewed with the faculty with whom she would be working. There had been nothing but her application and some letters of recommendation from her professors at DU to recommend her to the job. She had been offered only a temporary position working under Professor Frederick Shipley on a trial basis. That part of the offer letter hadn't popped out at her when she first read it in the garden shed. And she had already announced her new job to everyone and their brother by the time she figured out those stipulations. After that, she'd been too embarrassed to tell anyone the whole truth.

Sofia watched two students walk so close to the fountains that water droplets sprinkled across their shirts, leaving little wet spots spattered over the cloth. Her eyes followed the water to its peak where it fell over itself in a turmoil of bubbled spheres before falling back to earth. The towering Bush House stood on the other side of the fountains, beckoning her to enter and face her fate.

"Well, no going back now," Sofia said to herself under her

breath. She loved math, she had to remember that. The logic of it. The way it was forced to do the right and correct thing no matter what. Math didn't change its mind because of emotion. It didn't lie. It didn't change. It made the whole world make sense. "All you have to do is your best," she told herself. Then, before she lost her nerve, she straightened her shoulders and turned toward the entrance.

After climbing the magnificent staircase made of carved marble curving gracefully up from the front lobby, Sofia arrived at the third floor. She found her way down long hallways that crisscrossed through the huge building in an almost never-ending maze. When she finally found room 327 she hesitated before opening the substantial wooden door. The worn brass doorknob was smooth and cold to the touch. She took a deep breath through her nose and out through her mouth to quell her butterflies, then pushed the door open.

Sofia had spent hours researching this position as well as her new boss, Professor Shipley. He was an expert in his field of math and data analytics. She had online stalked him and found pictures of him at several university websites where he had presented his research, as well as on King's College website. Some of his better known lectures had even made it to YouTube. From all of this she had learned a few things about him. He was 67 years old, held three doctorate degrees in mathematical sciences, lived in London currently, but had been born in Liverpool. He was not only intellectually intimidating, but had a towering physical presence as well. Of a hefty stature, 6' 5" tall, and with a deep, commanding voice, he was one of the most successful black men in his field.

With these expectations front of mind, it was no wonder Sofia was surprised to find an entirely different individual waiting for her on the other side of the door. Instead of a tall older black man, Sofia found a tall, platinum haired white woman perched on the corner of a long table in the center of the room. The woman was in her fifties, had thin almost white hair that fell limp and straight to just past her broad chin. Her eyes were small and narrow, and her face was long, reminding Sofia of a horse. When the woman saw her she stood and smiled, revealing very large horse like teeth. When she spoke her voice was deep and smooth.

"You must be Dr. Venegas," the woman said, offering Sofia her hand.

Sofia answered as confidently as she could manage, "Yes, yes I am." She took the woman's hand to shake. Her hand was so big it wrapped completely around Sofia's with room to spare.

"I'm Professor Weston, Clara Weston," the woman said as she shook Sofia's hand firmly.

It took a moment for the name to register. "Oh yes, of course, Dr. Weston," Sofia said. She had read up on Dr. Clara Weston as well. "I'm familiar with your work."

"Please, call me Clara. I get enough of the 'doctor' and 'professor' thing from students."

Much of Sofia's nerves settled as Clara showed her around the suite of rooms. Clara had her own office and Professor Shipley had a larger office next to hers. Both office doors connected to the large room that held the long table where Clara had been sitting when Sofia arrived. There were several laptops on the table and two desktop computers on small tables up against one wall. There was a long window on the other wall that looked out over the courtyard and the fountains. The floors were all dark wood and shone as if they'd been buffed a thousand times, which was probably the case. Comfortably cool despite the warm August morning, the room had that slight sour scent that accompanied all old buildings.

"We've set up a workstation for you here," Clara motioned Sofia toward what could only be described as a dent in the wall, a four-by-four space that may have at one time been a closet but now had no door. The architectural feature created a cramped cubby where a small desk, lamp, desktop computer and office chair could fit–barely. "It may feel a bit cramped here," Clara said apologetically. "But much of the time you'll be working at the larger table with the grad students. So hopefully this will work." Clara's long, bland face gave Sofia a hopeful smile.

"Yes, it will be just fine, thank you," Sofia responded politely. She tried to give Clara a warm smile, but she was a little disappointed not to get her own office. Even a small office would have gone a long way to making her presence here feel more permanent.

"And this is where we make our tea," Clara added brightly, sweeping her long arm toward an antique secretary a few feet away from Sofia's new chair. The left side was a glass cabinet, which held china teacups. The flat surface on top of the cabinet held an electric teapot, and on the right side, on the shelf in front of a beveled mirror, was a real china sugar bowl and a handful of stir sticks in a yellow glass jar. Clara pulled down the shelf where a fine lady may have penned a letter 150 years or more ago. Instead of stationary and inkwell, the shelves inside held several types of tea.

"On a break again, are we?" A booming voice came from the front door.

Sofia knew without looking that this must be Professor Shipley. His voice had a proprietary air, plus she recognized it from the online videos. He loomed in the doorway holding a crooked stack of books in his arms. Sofia's nerves returned as she faced him.

"Frederick, this is Dr. Venegas," Clara introduced Sofia.

Bravely sticking out her hand, Sofia said, "Please, call me Sofia."

Professor Shipley moved into the room, scowling. He

stopped directly in front of her and Sofia had to practically look straight up in order to meet his irritated glare. He peered down at her outstretched hand through thick, black-rimmed glasses. Then he indicated the books filling his arms by lifting them slightly higher. His hands were full. As he dropped his arms back down he did something that Sofia had only imagined famous professors ever did. He made a *harrumph* sound.

"And you may call me Professor Shipley," he said. "Or Dr. Shipley." He brushed past her and after an awkward moment she returned her outstretched hand quickly to her side.

"Oh, Frederick," Clara said chiding.

Professor Shipley turned halfway back to the two women with an even deeper scowl darkening his expression. "You see, Clara, that's the problem. This informal tone you propagate will be the ruin of us all." Then he stomped into his office and used his foot to slam the door behind him.

Chapter Five

Her first few days at work were grueling. Sofia had never been so tired. Given the fact that she had worked her way through college, graduate school, and finally earned her PhD, the fact that this job was wiping her out certainly said something. What, she wasn't sure.

Clara was kind, intelligent, and patient. All of the students called her 'Dr. Clara' and Sofia found it more natural to call her that as well. The graduate students on Sofia's team, Henry and Liza, were both mild mannered math, science geeks. They were pale and thin with dark hair and looked like bookends. Even their mannerisms were the same. Quiet, smart, and efficient. If Sofia hadn't known better she would have guessed they were siblings. Everyone was quite nice and professional, except for Professor Shipley. Professor Shipley was a bear.

Whenever she felt like she was relaxing into the work, or they had reached an acceptable conclusion, or she was starting to feel like maybe taking this job and moving across the world wasn't the worst mistake of her life, Professor Shipley stuck his nose in and wreaked havoc on her day. He was demanding, condescending, and grumpy in every single interaction she had with him. At times she wondered if he had it in for her, but then backtracked on that thought. She was not the only one. Henry and Liza were terrified of him, as was every secretary or student or professor who interacted with him. Dr. Clara was the only one who seemed to be able to let everything he said roll off her back, like water off of a duck.

"I think of it as he expends so much energy using his brain that he has nothing left to manage his social interactions," she explained to Sofia one lunch break.

"I guess," Sofia responded with little to no conviction. She wanted to say something much more scathing, but didn't dare. She marveled at Dr. Clara's ability to say anything even remotely kind about him. The best thing Sofia could say about Professor Shipley was that he was consistent. Consistently a jerk.

At the end of her first week Sofia stopped at the liquor store and picked up three bottles of wine.

"One for tonight, one for Saturday, and one for Sunday," she said to herself as she was walking home. Her feet hurt from wearing high heels all week. Her eyes hurt from the strain of staring at numbers and computer screens all day. And her head hurt, because...well, just because.

When she got back to her flat Sofia kicked off her shoes and turned on the fan in her window for some air movement. Then she opened the first bottle of wine. She had made it one week and though it hadn't been the smoothest week of her life, she was still standing. It was time to have a mini-celebration.

When she sat down with her mug full of wine, she noticed that her phone had some messages. Texts from Luna, Bridget, Angie and Thomas, and three voicemails. She had been too sleepy the night before to check her voice mails so she clicked on those first.

The first one was her mother checking in on her. She

would have to call her back over the weekend and give her all of the news. The next message was from Tawnyetta.

"Exciting news!" Tawnyetta's voice rose from her speaker phone. "We're throwing a huge fundraiser for the health clinics and child care programs in our area. And guess what? It's going to be another ball, Sofia!" Sofia smiled. She could hear the excitement in Tawnyetta's voice. She had to agree, another ball at the Scottish Castle sounded pretty exciting. "So, anyway, we are going to be in London for a few days making some of the arrangements. We would love to see you while we're there. See your new place and everything. Call me! Hope your first week at work is going well! Talk to you later!"

Sofia took a sip of wine and made a mental note to call Tawnyetta this weekend, too. She deleted the message and hit the button to listen to her last voicemail.

A man's voice. She didn't recognize it right away, but the instant she did a shiver went across her shoulders. "Hi Sofia, it's Ian. Ian Law?" From the dinner party at Travis and Bea's? I certainly hope you remember me or this is even more wretched than it feels." Sofia's stomach did a flip-flop. He must have gotten her number from Bea. "I'm ringing you because I was wondering if you'd like to go out with me some-time? I know you're new to the area and I was thinking I could show you around...take you to see some of the sights...that sort of thing." The thrill of a possible new romance tickled her and she smiled. He sounded so nervous. So earnest. So sexy. "I'll just leave my number...oh, you probably already have it on your phone...but just in case you blocked it or something...I don't know why I said that...I doubt that you would block my number immediately...that would be harsh," There was a pause when she imagined he was wishing he could stop talk-ing. Then it started again, "I'm going to run out of–" The message ended. Her voicemail had cut him off.

She looked at her phone and considered her options. It

would be fun to go out with a cute guy and see the sights of London. He was definitely interesting. On the other hand, she was exhausted and needed to rest up over the weekend. Plus there was her job. She didn't really have time for dating, not with Professor Shipley breathing down her neck. She couldn't afford to make any mistakes because she was too tired, or distracted.

Just then a sharp knock sounded on her door, startling her. She wasn't expecting anyone. Maybe it was Bea and Travis again? She put her wine down on the table next to her phone and went to the door. She froze as the possibility of Ian coming right to her house to ask her out crossed her mind. A tingle of excitement moved across her fingers as she reached for the doorknob.

"Surprise!"

Tawnyetta and Michael waited for her on the other side of the door wearing big, goofy grins.

"Oh my God!" Sofia exclaimed, grabbing them both in a big hug.

"Did you get my message?" Tawnyetta asked.

"Yes, I just got it actually. I forgot to check my messages until tonight. But I didn't realize you were coming so soon!"

"Are you busy?" Michael asked. "I told Tawnyetta not to get her hopes up in case you had other plans."

"No, not at all," Sofia shook her head 'no' as she ushered them in. A flicker of disappointment passed through her. She couldn't call Ian back now that she had company. Just as quickly as the thought came she brushed it away.

"This is adorable!" Tawnyetta said as she walked around the tiny flat. She spread her arms out like model on a game show presenting the newest, biggest prize.

"And so close to the university," Michael added as he peered out her window.

"It is convenient for sure," Sofia said. "Certainly not as big as what you're used to," she added, teasing.

She offered them a glass of wine and they told her they had come to whisk her off to dinner.

"I'll be the envy of every man in the room," Michael said in his most gallant Scottish accent.

He was gallant, that was for sure. Tall, dark, and handsome, Michael was every woman's dream in the looks department. He had piercing blue eyes and with that Scottish accent he could make any woman swoon. His charms had worked their magic on Tawnyetta and even though they'd been married for over a year Sofia could see the love shining in Tawnyetta's eyes every time she looked at him. It was so nice to have company and get to go out with old friends.

Sofia and Tawnyetta freshened up while Michael called for a taxi. Then, true to his word, he offered them both an arm and escorted them down the stairs and out to an evening on the town.

Sofia wasn't sure how wealthy one had to be to own a castle and be a lord like Michael MacBrody. He did not shy away from spending money throughout the evening, which was fun, but it also made her feel a little guilty. They had come to see her and were technically her guests, which would normally mean dinner would be her treat. But with her career balancing on a wire and after the expense of moving all the way to the UK, Sofia knew it was better to let Michael and Tawnyetta splurge on her. She tried to be gracious and accept it without guilt as she knew it was given freely.

In addition to being excited to see her safely in London, Tawnyetta was over the top excited about their upcoming fundraiser ball.

"We've decided to use the draw of the castle and whatever influence Michael's position has to address some of the social problems in our area," she explained over dinner.

"That's wonderful," Sofia said.

"It's all her idea," Michael said proudly. "My wife has a mind for helping others." He beamed at her as he said it, obviously proud of Tawnyetta's enthusiasm.

"We're getting as many famous and influential people as we can involved," Tawnyetta continued. But we're also utilizing the connections of people that aren't bigwigs. We don't want it to be snobby." She thought of something and touched Sofia's arm. "Do you remember that travel writer I met on the plane that I told you about, Clark? He's going to help with the PR for all of it, get it into the news and everything like that."

"That sounds great," Sofia answered as she lifted her wine glass to her lips and took a sip.

"And Michael's friend, Ian, do you remember him? He was the singer at our reception?"

Sofia swallowed the wine too fast, shocked at the mention of Ian's name. "Yes, yes I do remember him." If it had just been Tawnyetta she would have told her immediately about dinner with Ian and the message he had just left on her phone. But with Michael there she felt a little shy about it all, so she just smiled calmly.

"Well," Tawnyetta continued, "he's going to perform. He's really good, actually. Their band is getting a lot of recognition lately."

Sofia nodded and continued with her Mona Lisa Smile.

"I was curious," Tawnyetta added. "If you would feel comfortable inviting the professors you're working with and some others from King's College. People like that have a lot of influence and we would love to have them at the ball."

Sofia's stomach clenched. Professor Shipley at a ball? At a party? The two ideas didn't mesh well in her mind. Besides she didn't know if she was up to asking him such a question. Anything she said to him might send him over the edge and her into unemployment. Pretending that this was the best idea ever, Sofia tried to look positive.

"I can definitely work on that," she said in the most decisive non-committal way she could.

"Excellent! I'm so excited," Tawnyetta gushed. She put one hand on Sofia's hand and one on Michael's and squeezed them warmly. "This is going to be great!"

Sofia did her best to keep up her mood, but she was not so sure she agreed with Tawnyetta's declaration at all.

Chapter Six

The next morning Sofia got up bright and early. Tawnyetta and Michael had several meetings scheduled throughout the day and wouldn't be available for socializing until this evening. That was just as well with Sofia, because she had several Saturday chores she wanted to get out of the way.

First and foremost, she needed to do her laundry. With only a laundromat, but no dry cleaners, nearby and being unwilling to spend the money for pickup and delivery from a dry cleaners further away, Sofia spent the first part of her morning washing her delicates in her bathroom sink. After carefully squeezing them dry she hung all of them from the shower curtain rod, towel racks, and even the doorknobs to dry. When she was done, all of her unmentionables, including underwear, bras, tights, slips, camisoles, and two of her lacy baby doll nighties, filled every possible space in the tiny bathroom. She opened the minuscule bathroom window for more air movement to help them dry and moved on to the rest of her laundry.

Her tiny flat came equipped with a mini stacked washer and dryer in what she originally thought was a pantry, but turned out to be the laundry closet, right in the middle of her kitchen. She supposed it was a luxury to be able to do laundry in her flat at all, even if she had to do it in several small loads so as not to overstuff the washing machine. She sorted her laundry into four small piles on the kitchen floor and put the first one in to wash.

After that was done Sofia grabbed her purse and two canvas shopping bags and left to get some groceries. Unlike back in Denver where she would take one trip in her car to a giant supermarket, here she wandered along charming sidewalks and ducked into each small specialty shop to purchase her groceries one or two items at a time. The bakery called to her first with its mouth-watering smell of bread baking wafting down the street. She picked up two crusty French loaves and some scones to go with her morning coffee. Next was the cheese shop, then the butcher shop, then a fresh fruit, vegetable and flower shop. She decided to splurge on an inexpensive bouquet of sunflowers for her table, since the bouquet Tawnyetta had sent her was past its prime.

Laden down with her purchases she headed back to her flat, but stopped when she came across a candy shop cleverly decorated to look like a gingerbread house.

"Good morning, dearie, what can I get you today?" A small, round faced woman asked once Sofia got herself and her overflowing canvas bags through the door.

Sofia looked around at the shelves of large glass candy jars, each with a shining tin lid, and filled with every shape, color, and type of candy imaginable.

"Gosh," Sofia answered, feeling a little out of her element. "I don't really know where to begin."

The round-faced proprietor noticed her accent. "American, are you?"

"Yes," Sofia answered.

"Well now, would you like some suggestions on the best British sweeties?"

Sofia did. The gingerbread shop owner was happy to oblige and sent her home with a few Double Decker candy bars, Pear Drops, and a small tin of Turkish Delight–just like in Chronicles of Narnia.

Once home Sofia put away the perishables in her almost dorm sized refrigerator. Lastly, she tossed the old bouquet and arranged her sunflowers in the vase they had occupied, placing them in the center of her kitchen table.

Satisfied with her work for the day, Sofia decided it was time for a snack and a little relaxation with one of the books she'd bought at the Red Lion bookstore last week. Pulling out a plate from the cupboard, she arranged a piece of Camembert, slices of hard salami, a chunk of French bread, and a couple of fresh strawberries to eat while she read. She added a handful of Pear Drops as dessert and settled into her couch. The morning had been overcast, but not rainy. The sun was beginning to poke its head out of the clouds promising a nice afternoon and evening.

Nestled into her couch with the plate of munchies on the cushion next to her, she picked up her gently used copy of The Keeper of Lost Things. Before she started reading, she looked around at her surroundings and felt quite pleased with her accomplishments. She made a mental note to take Tawnyetta and Michael to the funny little bookstore. She knew Tawnyetta would love it as much as she did.

Maybe because of all of the activity of the week, or maybe because she had stayed out later than normal the night before with Tawnyetta and Michael, but before she had eaten much of her snack or even made it through the first chapter of her book, Sofia drifted off to sleep. The book fell open in her lap as her grip loosened. Her neck grew limp and her head fell softly to the side. Her body slumped sideways and slowly dropped to the cushions of the couch until she was laying with her cheek resting on her uneaten munchies. She remained that way, snoring quietly, completely undisturbed, until almost an hour later when a sudden sound woke her.

Knock. Knock. Knock.

Sofia sat up, startled, sending her book and the plate tumbling to the floor. Stale bread, warm Camembert, and dried slices of salami scattered at her feet. The knocking came again and Sofia tried to wake up. What time was it? Had she slept through the whole afternoon?

"Coming," she called out, but her voice was still thick with sleep. She cleared her throat and said again, "Coming."

Leaning over she scooped up the food off the floor and onto the plate. As she did, a piece of cheese, that had apparently been stuck to her cheek, fell off and plopped in a melted mess onto the floor.

"Sheesh," she said, shaking her head and chuckling at the ridiculousness of it. She wiped both hands over her face to ensure nothing else was stuck to her and got up. Tawnyetta and Michael were already there and she was far from ready. Still sleepy, she swayed a little as she deposited the plate of ruined snacks on the kitchen table and headed to the door.

"I'm sorry," she explained as she unlocked the door to open it. "I fell asleep!" As she opened the door she laughed at her discombobulation, "And I had a piece of cheese stuck to my face–" She stopped short. It wasn't Tawnyetta and Michael knocking at her door. It was Ian.

Ian, with his dark red punk style hair, worn-out jeans, gleaming golden eyes, sexy tattoos, and a big fat smile on his face.

"Hullo," he said. He said the greeting with an 'uh' instead of an 'eh'. It was cute. Really, really cute.

Sofia blinked a few times, not sure she was seeing what was right in front of her. Then, realizing he was waiting for a response, she said, "I thought you were someone else."

"Fair enough," he nodded. His cat eyes sparkled with merriment and Sofia felt as if a small earthquake was moving the floor under her feet. Her confusion caused by being woken from a deep sleep was magnified by not understanding exactly why he was there. Her brow creased with that question, but she didn't ask it.

Instead she said, "I got your message."

"Right, that," he said. He shifted uncomfortably from one foot to the other before screwing up his brow with concern. "Sorry...is this weird?" He shoved one hand into the front pocket of his jeans and crumpled his shoulders forward in pure embarrassment. "I just realized that this might be really, really weird. Considering the message I left you and all of that. I don't...I mean...I do have a perfectly legitimate reason for stopping by. But now I'm thinking from your perspective it might not seem legitimate at all. I'm not stalking you or anything like that, in case you were wondering..." His voice trailed off. He lifted his other arm up so she could see he was holding a purple sweater. Her purple sweater. "I was at Bea and Travis' last night helping Travis do some carpentry work...you know men fixing plumbing nonsense. Bea said she was going to drop your sweater by because you left it the other night and I told her I would be happy to drop it by since I live closer. You know...save them a trip?"

Sofia's own confusion dissipated as she watched Ian fumble for words and try to explain why he was at her front door. If he had been a complete stranger and was unknown to any of her friends she may have found him showing up at her door a little strange, true. However, he was a friend of Bea and Travis, and he was a college friend of Michael's, and she had spent an entire evening with him and found him to be charming. Nothing about him screamed 'creepy'.

Her emerald eyes narrowed and she looked him up and down as if deciding his fate. In a way she was, she supposed. Even though he dressed a little rough and was tatted up, and was probably a lot wilder than most of her friends and family, something about Ian Law made Sofia feel like taking a chance.

"I guess it's not too weird," she said with a smile.

Her words released him from the grip of self-doubt. He returned her smile with one that started in his eyes and spread across his entire face. Her body tingled in response.

"Fantastic, great!" He pushed the sweater toward her. "Here you are then." She took the sweater. Ian shoved his free hand into his other pocket and rocked back and forth on his feet. "So...I'll be going," he said, to her surprise. "Let me know if you decide you'd like to see some sights with me. No pressure or anything." He backed away a few steps then turned to make an escape down the hall.

"Wait," she said. He stopped, turned, and waited, an uncertain smile stuck to his face. "Thank you for bringing this," she said. "Would you like to come in?"

Relief. He grinned, "I would, thank you."

After several minutes of Ian complementing her flat, she knew for sure that he was completely harmless. Despite his rebellious look, he tried hard to be extremely polite and was careful not to offend. In fact, he tried so hard it hurt.

"Nice view," he said as he looked appreciatively out the window. He nodded as he took a second look. "Lots of light and fresh air." He looked at her bookshelf, nodding in approval. "Nice bookshelf."

She wondered if he had to be extra sweet in life to counteract people's reaction to all of his tattoos. When she'd first seen him at the dinner party, Sofia had been too polite to look closely at them. Now that he was doing most of the talking and she felt a little more comfortable with him, she let her eyes wander down some of the images.

One arm had a line of sheet music twisting up from the top of his left hand, around his arm and disappearing under the sleeve of his T-shirt. Under the musical notes were lyrics written in script, but she couldn't read what they said. The other arm had a series of skulls and clocks and crowns. Throughout both arms were different sized red roses, black roses, and red and black hearts. Some with banners and words, some without. Add to that his choice of jewelry, which consisted of two chunky silver rings on his right hand and several wood bead bracelets on his left wrist, he definitely had the musician look down.

"Do you mind terribly if I use your loo?" Ian asked. Sofia paused. She had to translate his meaning, which he took as a sign she thought the request odd. "It's just that it took me a little while to find your place, walking up and down the halls."

"Yes, of course," she answered and told him where to find the bathroom.

He left the room and Sofia's gaze fell on her book that still lay discarded on the floor. She went to pick it up and as she bent down she noticed her piles of dirty clothes resting on the kitchen floor. Hurrying over, she pushed them with her foot into the laundry closet, shutting the flimsy door to hide them from sight.

Satisfied, Sofia turned away from the laundry. That's when it hit her. Her delicates. She had sent Ian into her bathroom that was draped with all of her most intimate apparel. She fought the urge to run to the bathroom. What was she going to do? Fling the door open and interrupt him?

She heard the door of the bathroom open and could do nothing but face Ian as he returned. At first he didn't say anything and she wondered if by some miracle she had put everything away in her sleep.

Ian moved to the counter next to where she stood by the laundry closet. He leaned casually against it and crossed his arms in front of him, nodding to himself as he did. He lifted his eyes to hers. They were dancing.

"Nice bathroom," he said.

"Oh my God," Sofia covered her face with her hands, laughing. "I'm so sorry, I forgot they were in there!"

Ian lifted his eyebrows at her and stuck out his bottom lip as if considering her apology. "Don't be sorry, Sofia," he bumped her shoulder softly with his own. "That's the nicest bathroom I've ever seen."

Though she laughed at his comment, she could barely look at him. "I'm mortified," she said into her hands.

"No, no, don't be mortified," his British accent made this entreaty that much more appealing.

Gathering her courage, she checked to see if he was sincere. His eyes sparkled with humor and an intimacy she couldn't explain considering the short time they had known each other. Flustered, she tried to look away, but couldn't.

"Really, truly, it's not a bad thing at all," he nudged her again with his shoulder. "I know!" He interrupted her mortification with an idea. "Let's go get something to eat. I'm famished." He stepped over to the kitchen table and grabbed a piece of the hard salami she'd picked up off the floor to pop into his mouth.

"No!" Sofia lunged forward as she shouted. Ian froze with his hand mid-air, baffled at her reaction. "Sorry," she put her hand over his hand that held the salami and pressed on it, pushing it back down to the plate. "That's not edible," she explained, but the words had become unimportant because as she touched his hand she saw the confusion on his face turn into something more, an intense attraction. She recognized it on him, because she was experiencing the same feeling.

"What do you say?" Ian asked, his voice low. He let the piece of salami drop back on the plate, but she found it impossible to take her hand from where it rested on his.

"I can't," she said quietly and watched disappointment cloud his eyes. "I have plans already. I'm sorry," she said, and she meant it.

Suddenly, her cell phone rang. They both jumped at the sound, as if they'd been caught in a clandestine moment.

Tearing herself away from him, Sofia pulled her phone out of her purse. It was Tawnyetta.

"Hello?" She answered, turning away but seeing Ian watch her as she did.

"Guess what?" Tawnyetta asked.

"What?"

"We're hung up in this meeting and it doesn't look like we're going to get back until late. We won't be able to do anything tonight with you," Tawnyetta said apologetically.

Sofia faced Ian and he caught her in his gaze. Her cell phone volume was on high and she could tell from his expression that he had heard Tawnyetta.

"No?"

"I'm sorry, Sofia," Tawnyetta continued.

"Don't worry about it," Sofia said as a slow smile spread over Ian's face.

She hit the 'End' button on her phone. A feeling of anticipation was palpable in the room.

Sofia cleared her throat as she said, "My plans have been cancelled."

Ian nodded, trying to be nonchalant. "I gathered that."

"So..."

"So..." He cocked his head at her, his handsome bad boy

look irresistible. "Since you're free...will you let me take you out?"

Heat filled her cheeks and she looked down coyly. "Yes," she answered.

Ian leaned forward, so close she could have touched his tattoos with the tips of her fingers. When he spoke, his voice whispered over her cheek and lips, sending a shiver down her spine. "I promise, you're not going to regret this."

Chapter Seven

When Ian promised her an evening she would never forget, Sofia had not expected it would start on the corner of a busy street.

Just before they left her flat she had changed out of her Saturday chore clothes into a cream colored sundress with the thinnest pattern of white swirls on the fabric. The dress was well tailored, light and airy, and complemented her rich brown skin. She pulled her hair back into a long braid that fell down to the middle of her back and put on her favorite pair of sexy, white sandals. When she came out of her bedroom Ian was leaning casually against her counter, waiting. When he saw her he straightened up and stared at her for a few beats, surprised and pleased at the way she looked. That had made her feel good, but later as she sat on the street corner waiting for him, Sofia felt woefully overdressed.

Ian had abandoned her briefly on an iron bench that was positioned in the shade of a building while he waited in the long line to get their meal. Fish and chips from a street cart that he swore by. It took him a good twenty minutes, five of it he spent chatting up the gentleman who ran the food cart. They looked like old friends the way they were going on with each other.

Never in her life had someone asked her out on a date and not taken her someplace with valets...or at least waiters. Not once. Not ever. For the full twenty minutes he was getting their food Sofia racked her brain trying to think of a less impressive first date experience in her past. She came up empty.

"Tuck in, you're going to need your energy," he said when he returned and handed her a heaping serving of deep fried battered fish and what she thought of as French fries, but were called chips in the UK. The massive amount of food was wrapped like a bouquet of flowers in paper made to look like newsprint. This helped soak up the grease, hopefully. Sofia held the monstrous meal away from her body so grease wouldn't spill on her dress.

"Thank you," she said politely. She tried to mask her dismay.

"Now, now," Ian said, reading her expression. "Don't be disappointed before you try it."

She picked up a chunk of the piping hot fish and broke off a piece. Steam lifted from the flaky white fish inside. He did the same and put the whole piece into his mouth. Sofia bit into the crispy deliciousness. The fish tasted light and mild, with a satisfying crispy chewiness from the deep-fried batter. Tangy, sweet, delicious. Her mouth still full she looked at Ian with wide eyes. This was far better than she expected. She couldn't speak with her mouth full, but she tried to smile at him.

"Did I tell you or did I tell you?" Ian grinned and took another generous bite.

They shared the bench as they ate every morsel of the

delectable street food. Full and satisfied, all that remained of their dinner was the greasy newspaper wrapping it came in. Ian took hers, crumpled them both up into paper balls and tossed them into a nearby trashcan as if he was shooting basketball. He scored twice in a row.

"Are you thirsty?" he asked. She got the feeling this was a loaded question. Sofia nodded. Standing up and offering her his hand, he asked, "Fancy a pint?" 90% sure she knew what he was asking, Sofia nodded again.

She took his hand and he pulled her swiftly up so they were standing chest to chest. She liked how small her hand felt wrapped in his and she became very aware of his personal space. For a moment she wondered what it must be like to kiss someone like Ian Law. Her eyes dropped to his mouth then shot back up so he wouldn't guess what she was thinking.

"Ready then?" he asked. A true gentleman. But lingering behind those cat eyes she saw a flicker of amusement and knew instantly that he had guessed exactly what she was thinking.

"I'm ready," she answered. They strolled down the street still holding hands while Ian gave her a guided tour, complete with colorful anecdotes.

"My Nan used to shop here. She made all of her own dresses, and my mum's, and my sister's, before she died," he told her as they passed a sewing and needlework shop. He pointed at Sofia's favorite bakery with his chin as they walked by. "My brother stole a cookie from this place when he was eight years old. My mum made him come back everyday for the whole summer and help the old man who ran the place clean up at the end of the day."

"Really? I love this place."

"I think the old man passed away years ago. His son runs it now."

"You grew up around here?"

Ian nodded and pointed up the street. "If you go to Chestnut and turn left, then four streets down turn right on Rose Avenue, one more and take a left on Swallow Street, then three buildings up on the right, fourth floor, second door on the left. That's where I grew up."

Sofia laughed.

"What?"

"That's a very precise answer," she chuckled.

He grinned. "How's this for you, then? When you walk in the front door hang your jacket up on the left, boots off please if it's been raining, turn the corner to the right and say 'Hi' to Mum who's sitting there watching the telly, quick left, up fourteen stairs," here he paused and wrinkled his brow as if trying to remember. Sofia responded with another giggle. "Ah, yes! Second door on the right, and you're there straight away."

"That's your room?"

"Well, it was my room when I was an impressionable young man," he admitted. They walked along for a few minutes quietly before Ian asked, "Do you like precise answers?"

Sofia studied him as she pondered the question. It seemed an odd thing to ask. Even more odd was that it carried with it an insight about the way her mind worked. "Yes, I do."

"Makes sense, what with you making a career out of high math."

"I suppose it does," she smiled. "Do you?"

"Like precise answers?" he asked. She nodded and waited as he took his time considering the question. "Not complete-ly," he said, annunciating each consonant carefully. "I like loose ends, you know? I like a bit of freedom. I like not knowing exactly what's around the corner."

They continued making their way down the street, comfortably meandering and taking in all of the sights. The thought occurred to Sofia that Ian's love of freedom might mean that they were just going to wander around all night, finding refreshments at various street vendors. Maybe he hadn't made detailed plans. This thought made her feel strange. Was it wise for her to be out on the streets of London as the sun set lower in the sky wandering around with a man she barely knew? His grip on her hand that had felt so comforting and warm a few minutes ago changed into an uncomfortable link between them. She thought about how she could slip her hand out of his without causing a big scene.

"Here we are," Ian said as he abruptly stopped in front of a building that looked like it had been lifted out of the pages of a fairy tale book and plopped onto the street. A standalone building, barely, there couldn't have been more than six inches between its outside walls and the walls of the establishments on either side. A large wooden sign hung from an iron mast that stuck straight out from above the door.

Sofia read the sign out loud. "The Sneezing Pigeon..."

"In all her glory," Ian answered.

The Sneezing Pigeon was built with solid chunks of wood stacked like so many giant blocks. Painted in ox blood red and deep forest green, it had yellowed glass windows across the front, so frosted from age that nothing could be seen through them. Baskets of flowers hung from iron hooks embedded in the wall. Mounds of flowers also grew in window containers under each window, and in two long beds that were built between the Sneezing Pigeon and the sidewalk.

Sofia knit her brow and gave him an incredulous look. "The Sneezing Pigeon?"

"Absolutely," he answered.

The warm smell of yeast greeted her as Ian ushered her in. Fermentation of beer and ale, fresh baked bread, and meat stewing in a pot with onions and carrots, gave The Sneezing Pigeon a pleasant smell. Once her eyes adjusted to the dark interior, Sofia took in the long room. On one side there was a row of green paisley upholstered bench seating with wooden tables placed in line along them. The opposite side of the room was home to a long shining bar with plush red upholstered bar stools. Shelves and shelves of glass liquor bottles lined the wall behind the counter. On the far end of the room was a timeworn fireplace filling most of the wall, and a small stage stuck into the corner.

Ian entered behind her and instantly two of the men sitting at the bar called out to him in greeting. He lifted his hand to wave, but did not make a move to sit by them. Although Sofia could not see where else they might take a seat, all of the tables were full of patrons.

"Oi, Rupert," Ian called out. Sofia followed his gaze to see a heavyset balding man who dominated most of the space behind the bar.

"Ian!" Rupert called back, shifting his eyes momentarily to give her a quick nod of greeting, then back to Ian.

"Anything in back?" Ian asked.

"She's all yours," Rupert motioned to an open doorway next to the fireplace that Sofia hadn't noticed at first glance.

Everything was shiny brass and polished wood in this place. Green and gold tinted glass shades were on all of the lamps and a familiar uneven feeling under her feet that reminded her of the Red Lion Bookstore. As they went to the back they were surrounded by the sounds of clinking glasses, low laughter, and murmurs of conversation. As soon as she stepped into the back she let out a sigh of relief. Cool air welcomed her in this cave like room. Damp, dark comfort, as if it had been carved out of this space since the beginning of time and offered a safe reprieve from the outside world.

Their table was small and round. Intimate. Two chairs, two glasses of cool amber ale with creamy foam froth on top.

"You may laugh at the name," Ian said as he lifted the glass to his lips. "But The Sneezing Pigeon serves the best pints in London."

Sofia sipped the cold bitter liquid. It ran over her tongue and down her throat. The bitterness quenched her thirst more than something sweet. This was the perfect complement to their dinner.

Lighting in the back room was even darker than the front. Scant wall sconces glowing dimly did little to alleviate the problem so The Sneezing Pigeon also had votive candles lit, one on each table. She watched Ian in the candlelight as he took a healthy swallow of his ale and wiped the froth off of his upper lip with the back of his hand. As he dropped his hand back to the table in front of her, Sofia's eyes followed.

Her brow pinched together in a question. "What does your tattoo say?" She let her finger drop to the very beginning of his sheet music tattoo, which started on his hand and twisted up and around his forearm, disappearing under his T-shirt. Her nails were painted a rose pink and she watched his eyes follow her finger as she traced the first word, 'Whisper...'

Finally, he lifted his eyes to hers and held them for a moment. They were darker in this light. A chill began at the base of her neck and moved deliciously down her spine as he looked into her eyes. The ale was working fast.

Ian left his hand resting under her finger as if the weight of it was holding his hand against the table. With his other hand he pulled the sleeve of his shirt up, twisting his torso sideways so she could follow the tattoo as it wrapped like a rope around the muscles of his arm.

"Whisper words of wisdom..." he read it to her.

"Let it be? The Beatles?"

"The Beatles...always," he grinned. Before she could react, Ian leaned forward, both arms on the table, and sang the first few lines of the song to her. Sofia sat in silence letting his voice move over her like liquid. His breath, tinged with the bitter ale, brushed against her cheeks and a swell of attraction over-took all of her other senses.

She swallowed, hard.

Ian was so close to her she could smell his cologne. The same cologne he'd worn at the dinner party. Captivating. A crooked smile crept across his face as he watched her gaze move languidly along the hard lines of his jaw to his thick, red hair, before resting on his surreal eyes.

"I–" she started. The glimmer in his eyes, so sensual, so intense, interrupted her thought. What had she been about to say? She couldn't remember.

He lifted both eyebrows at her. "You...what?" His voice was deep, relaxed.

Sofia dropped her gaze and saw that her hand was still on his. She pulled it away and sat back in her chair, breaking the spell. It suddenly seemed too warm in this room. Cramped. Stuffy.

"I think I need some fresh air," she said.

As soon as they stepped back onto the street Sofia felt more like herself. Solid ground under her feet, the early evening air cool and refreshing. She felt awake, alert. It had been good to get out and spend some time with someone new. Someone from her new city who was very cute and interesting. A casual date was probably exactly what she had needed to take the edge off of her first week at work and feel a little more comfortable in her new surroundings.

They turned in the direction of her flat.

"This has been really nice, Ian," Sofia said. She wanted to compliment him on his interesting choices and make sure he knew she appreciated his effort.

"Has it?"

She looked at him sideways as they walked together. "Yes, great fish and chips and an authentic English pub," she added. "Thank you for showing me around."

Ian stopped and turned to her. "It's eight o'clock."

Sofia stopped and faced him, confused over his meaning. "Yes?"

"Are you ready to go home?"

Sofia glanced around, looking for anything else date-like to do on the sidewalk. The early evening had turned to the soft twilight of night around them. Street lights had turned on and the bustle of the city had a less business feel, more like a night out. She lifted her shoulders in a meek shrug. "I do have work on Monday."

Ian coughed out a laugh. "It's Saturday!"

"I thought...I mean," she fumbled for words.

Concern filled his eyes. "Do you want to go home? If you want to go home, I'll take you."

"No," she answered unconvincingly. She did want to go home, but not because she wasn't enjoying herself or enjoying Ian. Exactly the opposite, in fact.

Ian watched her face carefully. Being scrutinized so closely by those other worldly eyes made her feel young and bashful. She chewed her bottom lip uncertainly.

"Come on, then," he said, carefully taking her by the elbow and resuming their stroll. "I'll walk you to your flat if you like."

"No, no," she answered, with more clarity this time. "I just thought dinner and a drink was the whole evening," she tried to explain. "You're right, I don't *have* to go home now."

He lifted his brow and spoke in all seriousness, "You're certain?"

"Yes, I'm certain," she responded. But she wasn't certain at all. Agreeing to stay in Ian's company filled her stomach with butterflies and made her feel a little lightheaded.

He smiled. That smile. The one that started in his eyes and moved across his whole face. "Brilliant," he said. Ian looked past her to the street and raised his arm high in the air. Putting his tongue against his front teeth he let out a piercing whistle that stopped a nearby taxi. He stepped to the back door and opened it with a flourish. "You're coach, my lady," he swept his arm gallantly toward the dark interior of the cab. As she moved past him he winked at her, sending a flurry of butter-flies from her stomach into her chest. "I'll show you something you can't see anywhere else in the world," he said.

Chapter Eight

"A Ferris wheel?" Sofia stared up at the giant turning wheel hovering at the side of the Thames River. It was lit up like a carnival.

"No, not exactly," Ian explained. "It's actually a cantilevered observation wheel," he enunciated the words carefully. With his accent the description seemed even stranger.

"A what?"

"It's called the London Eye and it's not a Ferris wheel. It looks out over the city."

The structure of the thing was certainly more heavy duty than any Ferris wheel Sofia had ever been on. Two massive round struts lifted from the ground and came to a point in the center of the wheel. Those were its main support, but they seemed more the size of something a ship would need than a simple Ferris wheel. She had seen glimpses of the wheel on her walks along the Thames near her flat, but as they approached the massive contraption she could see it was much bigger up close.

"How tall is it?" she asked.

They moved past a sign giving instructions on where to buy tickets along with a few details. 135 meters, the sign said.

"135 meters," Ian told her with a cocky smile.

Meters. Sofia did a quick calculation in her head and her stomach clenched with apprehension. That was over 440 feet tall! She tilted her head back to see what she could see of the very top of the turning wheel. 32 pods made of glass and totally enclosed were dotted around the edge. Full of people, they reminded her of gondolas she'd ridden at ski resorts. Equipped with sliding doors, the pods dangled over the Thames River, letting people off then new riders on before closing and lifting slowly back into the air.

"You're not afraid of heights are you?" Ian's question was sincere.

"Not yet," she answered.

There were lines to buy tickets as well as kiosks where people were picking up tickets they had purchased online. Ian went for neither of these possibilities. Instead he led her to the back side of an information booth where a young man and older woman wearing royal blue vests with name-tags over their shirts were answering questions.

"Ian!" The man said with pleased recognition.

"Evening, Eddie," Ian said chummily. "Got any extra tickets for me and the lady?"

Eddie smiled at Sofia while trying not to seem like he was looking at her too hard. Sofia smiled back and attempted not to feel looked at.

"That I have," Eddie said. He reached toward the ticket machine on his counter and pushed a few buttons. Two computer printed tickets pushed out of the slot. He handed them to Ian. "Here you go, mate." Ian pulled his wallet from his back pocket, but Eddie raised his palm and shook his head. "I won't take your money."

Ian lifted his hand in a half salute and said, "I'll get you back."

Eddie leaned toward them hopefully, "Any concerts coming up?"

"Of course, I'll put you on the list...plus one," Ian responded, pointing a finger at Eddie to punctuate his promise.

"Fantastic, that's all I wanted to hear," Eddie called after them.

They made their way to the line of people waiting to board. The area for patrons to wait in line was made of glass and steel pillars painted white. It led back and forth on an upward slope rather like the wheelchair accessible ramps that led into large buildings. The whole place looked very modern and almost sci-fi, with a little bit of a Willy Wonka glass elevator vibe.

Ian kept his hand on the small of her back as they maneuvered through the crowd and Sofia found his touch distracting. She kept an eye on the wheel as it turned and lifted the pods up-up-up into the night sky and thought about how high 400 feet really was. That was the equivalent of a 40-story building. Surrounded by glass and dangling over the water.

Reading her expression, Ian asked, "Are you nervous?"

"A little," Sofia answered. She crossed her arms in front of her chest, partly because of the slight chill in the evening air and partly because she was a bit more than just a little nervous. She wished the credentials of the engineers that built these thrilling modes of entertainment were on display as they waited in line. Maybe her nerves would be tamed by knowing for sure how smart the people who had built this were.

"It's extremely safe," Ian reassured her, his hand still flat on the small of her back, adding to the mix of excitement and fear she was experiencing.

"Have you been on it a lot?"

"Oh, yes," he said. "I come here a lot. Especially when I need to clear my head."

When it was their turn and they stepped into the slow moving pod it felt much like an escalator under Sofia's feet. Ian guided her to the far end where they could hold onto the handrail and their view would be unobstructed. A dozen other people entered the temperature controlled pod before the doors suctioned closed and they began to rise into the air.

Ian stood close to her, one hand on her back and the other firmly holding the handrail by her waist. She was glad. Her legs were unsteady and she didn't want to wobble on her heels and fall over. She gripped the handrail tightly with both hands knowing he was there to steady her if necessary.

Sofia felt a tremor in her stomach, then realized it was actually her cell phone buzzing in her purse. She had pulled it to the front of her to rest on the handrail. She reached in and got her phone, side glancing at Ian who was standing so close to her he could not help but see the text that had popped onto her screen.

It was from Thomas.

What's up Buttercup?

Her phone provided an image of Thomas' handsome, smiling face just under the text. She turned her face toward Ian and was almost close enough for her lips to graze his cheek.

"It's my friend," she explained.

"I see...Thomas," Ian said. His breath tickled her neck and ear. When she lifted her eyes to him, she saw a flicker of a challenge cross his face. "Boyfriend?"

She smiled coyly. "No, just a friend."

Conscious of Ian's gaze on her, she texted an answer.

I'm on the London Eye!

Thomas' answer buzzed almost immediately back.

What's that?

"Want to show him?" Ian asked.

Their glass pod was rising through a support system of heavy white painted steel. But the Thames and the lights of London beyond were just coming into view as they rose above.

Ian maneuvered her so the view was behind both of them, then he wrapped his arm around her waist and pulled her close. Sofia lifted her phone for a selfie, the feel of Ian's arm holding her firmly and the smell of his cologne made her giddy. They both grinned happily for the picture and she sent it to Thomas. She was going to have to answer a thousand questions from him and the girls, but it was a cute picture.

Ian pointed out landmarks as they rose higher and higher into the air.

"There's Big Ben...there's Westminster Abbey," he spoke into her ear from behind, for he had turned her back to look out of the glass but remained as close as they had been while taking the selfie. His arm was still wrapped around her waist and holding her to him. Sofia didn't mind the feel of his chest against her back or the sound of his voice in her ear or the tickle of his breath on her neck. They were all pleasant sensations that distracted her from the height they had climbed to over the Thames.

"There's your flat," Ian pointed into a group of buildings that Sofia couldn't define. "And there's where we are playing next weekend," he pointed into another cluster of buildings that she didn't recognize.

She turned halfway towards him, her lips once again almost grazing his cheek. "You have a concert next weekend?"

"I do, well we do, the Robot Tellers," he answered. He glanced casually into her eyes, but she could tell by the way he squeezed her waste a little tighter that he was nervous. "Will you come?"

They were nearing the top of the wheel. Ian had told her when they boarded that The London Eye was a 30-minute ride, so they were almost halfway through it. She turned her gaze toward the view and as she did she saw herself and Ian reflected dimly in the glass of their pod. Her black hair, dark complexion, green eyes and creamy sundress. Ian, pale and lean, dark red hair, tattoos contrasting against his light skin. Opposites, but they looked good together. She couldn't look away from his eyes, which were intently watching her reflection instead of looking at the lights below them.

Sofia wasn't sure about accepting his invitation. Nor was she sure if this date had been a wise idea. But as they locked eyes in their reflection she was helpless to deny him.

"I'd love to," she answered just as they hit the peak of The London Eye, floating more than 40 stories in the air.

Chapter Nine

Monday morning came barreling down on Sofia like a bull. After a whirlwind weekend which included not only the date with Ian on Saturday night, but a full day of socializing with Tawnyetta and Michael as they buzzed around London shopping and planning for their upcoming fundraiser ball, Sofia was exhausted when she sat down at her dent in the wall office nook.

"Would you like a cup of tea to start the day?" Liza asked.

Sofia nodded numbly. How had she allowed herself to get so wiped out? She could barely keep her eyes open as Liza plugged in the electric teakettle.

It wasn't just fatigue. Even a strong cup of tea on top of the half pot of coffee she'd downed at her flat this morning probably wouldn't help. Her problem wasn't completely due to not feeling rested after her weekend. Her problem was she couldn't shake the memories of how her date had ended on Saturday night.

Ian had walked her home, all the way up the stairs and to her door. He had not asked to come in and she had not invited him. But she had wanted to invite him.

"Thank you so much," she had told him while fingering her house key nervously. "I had a wonderful time."

Ian leaned against the wall next to her door. His eyes gleaming cat-like in both color and expression.

"My pleasure, Sofia," he answered. The way her name rolled off his tongue was enticing. He tilted his head, curiosity on his face. "Tell me one thing."

"Yes?"

"Did you have fun?"

She smiled. "Yes, I did." And that was the truth.

He pushed away from the wall and hooked his thumbs in his front pockets, observing her calmly. "But?"

"But...what?" she asked.

"But not enough to go out with me again?"

Heat had flushed through her cheeks then as it did again at her desk when she relived the memory.

"No need to make excuses," he had continued. "I recognize all the signs."

She tried to brush his assumption away. "What signs?"

Ian took a half step closer to her and looked down into her eyes. The nearness of him sent her senses swirling again and she clenched her jaw to control them. She was torn. Torn between him standing there with his rebel look, exuding a primal sexuality that was impossible to ignore, and the world she knew she would return to on Monday morning. King's College. The steady, logical, and sensible world of numbers and academia. A world she understood.

"Oh, there are signs," he had said softly. Surprisingly, his expression belied no disappointment, no broken pride. She wondered for a moment if, despite all of the indications she'd read that he was attracted to her, perhaps he didn't like her that much after all.

She suddenly wished that she'd tried harder to enjoy the

evening, to enjoy him. Then that thought was pushed away by bigger concerns.

"It's just that we're very different...I think. And I'm not really looking for a relationship," she tried to explain.

The corners of his mouth lifted into an amused smile. "So, marriage is off the table, is it?"

The shock value of his statement broke through her discomfort and she chuckled. "Definitely."

Ian stepped back and threw up his hands in mock defeat. "I did my best. You can't ask any more of a fellow than his best."

"This is true," she giggled.

"Then I guess it's off to London Bridge to ponder my inadequacies and question the worthiness of my existence." He was making the best out of an awkward situation, and Sofia appreciated him so much for it. He was almost halfway down the hall, walking backwards as he joked with her.

"Good night, Ian," she said with as much warmth and kindness as she could without giving him the wrong impression.

He stiffened, put his hand on his heart, and gave her a short bow. She felt a tiny twist inside of her heart. Then he remembered something and pointed at her with both hands. "The concert, though. You'll still come, won't you?"

Of course she would, she had promised.

She spent the rest of the night tossing and turning wondering if that had been the right thing to do. On Sunday she had watched Tawnyetta and Michael be as in love as two people who were ever in love, which made her happy for them, but miserable for herself. Not miserable exactly. More like conflicted. Confused. Maybe miserable was the right word.

Her confused, conflicted, miserable self sipped the tea Liza handed her and poured over her emails. In her position for just one week and she already had dozens and dozens of emails awaiting her response.

"Good morning, team!" Dr. Clara entered the office and placed a bakery box on the long conference table. "I've brought scones for your enjoyment." Dr. Clara moved gracefully through the room. Her large frame and unflinching good humor reminded Sofia of old cooking shows with Julia Child she had seen before her parents had paid for cable. Dr. Clara stopped and checked the watch on her wrist. Yes, she still wore a watch. Turning her long, pale face to Sofia, Liza and Henry, her beady eyes blinked three times. "By my watch we have almost three hours before Frederick's first class of the day is over. Let's see what we can accomplish before he returns."

Knowing this was equivalent to being warned that a tornado would hit their little research area in three hours. Sofia gratefully took a scone and sat down with the others to get to work. But try as she might, the memory of Ian backing down her hallway and making her promise to come to his concert kept running through her mind.

Her days overflowed with work. Every night she returned to her flat worn to the bone by the mental effort it took to try and impress Professor Shipley. Even though she and the others had burned their brain cells up running reports, testing mathematical theories, and reviewing data, they didn't come close to impressing him. In fact, they were all thankful to have merely kept their jobs.

"Do I look stupid?" Professor Shipley had asked them after storming out of his office and slamming a printed report down on the large table where they were working. None of them answered, assuming it was a rhetorical question. "Well, do I?" He bellowed, his bushy eyebrows raising high on his forehead, pushing the skin between his eyebrows and receding hairline into something resembling a Sharpei dog.

Dr. Clara wasn't there to buffer this outburst so Sofia,

being the next highest in seniority, answered him, "No, you don't, sir."

Professor Shipley's eyes were large and round behind his spectacles, even larger and rounder when he was shouting. His cheeks weren't exactly jowls, not yet, but they jiggled a little as he spoke. In anyone else Sofia may have found this charming or amusing. But not in Professor Shipley's case.

"Good. Next time do not waste your time and my time annotating inconsequential points on these reports. You are to look deeper and find the things that I cannot see at a glance. That is your job." He punctuated this statement with his customary 'harrumph' and stomped back into his office, the abused report crunched up in his hand.

Friday finally arrived. And with it, not only a chance to spend a few days out of the grumbling, complaining, and insulting company of Professor Shipley, but also a second invitation to dinner at Bea and Travis' lovely Hampstead home.

"Sofia, you look well," Travis greeted her warmly at the door.

"Thank you," she answered, though she knew he was being kind. She looked tired, but she appreciated the sentiment.

"So it's pretty bad?" Bea asked her later at the table as Sofia regaled them with Professor Shipley horror stories over lemon chicken and salad.

"It's a bit of a nightmare, really," Sofia admitted.

Travis nodded knowingly. "He has a terrible reputation as a professor and a boss. But, unfortunately, he has an excellent reputation as a genius as well." Smiling wryly he refilled her wine glass.

"Yes, there's that genius part," Sofia reluctantly agreed.

"Well, let's be glad it's the weekend then," Bea offered cheerfully. "What other plans do you have?

Sofia cringed. The Robot Tellers concert was tomorrow night and she'd promised to go, but she wasn't sure if she was up to it. She explained her predicament to Bea and Travis. This was turning into a regular therapy session.

"Get out!" Bea exclaimed. "You went on a date with Ian?!"

Sofia wrinkled her nose. "It was a kind of a spur of the moment thing."

Travis grunted, grabbing both her and Bea's attention.

"What?" Bea asked him.

"Nothing," Travis sipped his wine and avoided eye contact with them both.

Bea's eyes narrowed and she pointed at him, jokingly accusing him of treachery. "What do you know about this Travis Prescott?"

Sofia watched with interest. She wondered what he knew about it, too.

Travis tried to shrug his wife's suspicions off. "Nothing...really."

"Did Ian tell you?" Bea was incredulous.

"Not exactly," Travis admitted. He looked at Sofia apologetically. He was a soft-spoken man and she imagined speaking about romance in public was something he had done next to never during his life.

"What then?" Bea pressed.

He stammered and squirmed a little, but got the gist of the story out. Apparently Ian had expressed to Travis an interest in Sofia that went beyond wishing to be helpful by returning her sweater. He had told Travis that he thought she was 'quite comely' and 'a prospective romantic match', though Sofia suspected Travis was paraphrasing. She couldn't imagine Ian speaking quite that formally.

"And you didn't tell me?" Bea's voice hit a pitch that might be considered a low shriek. Travis cringed. "I can't believe you went matchmaking behind my back!" Bea was more incensed at being left out of the plotting than at the principle of the thing.

"It wasn't matchmaking," Travis told Sofia, ignoring his wife's outburst. "I didn't see any harm in letting him bring you your sweater." His big, droopy eyes looked at her dolefully. "Are you offended?"

Sofia dismissed the question with a wave of her hand. "No, that's not it," she tried to explain. "It's just that now I've promised to go to this concert and I feel uncomfortable. Like I'm encouraging him when I don't think we're a good match. I don't want him to think we're on another date."

Travis nodded with understanding, cheerlessly accepting her unfortunate circumstances. Bea, on the other hand, pooh-poohed that idea with a scoff.

"You can go with us," she announced.

"You're going?"

"Of course we're going. We're big fans of his. Friend-fans," she beamed at Sofia. "This way you can go enjoy the concert and it won't be weird and awkward, but you'll still be showing up like you promised." Bea patted Sofia's hand and stood up from the table to start collecting dishes. As she did she hummed merrily to herself, having solved the problem in her own mind. Travis stood to help his wife, avoiding looking at Sofia and therefore removing himself from the conversation. "Don't worry," Bea told her as she carried plates into the kitchen. "Everything will turn out just fine."

Sofia was not confident Bea's plan was as foolproof as she thought it was.

Chapter Ten

People of all ages filled the small venue to capacity. The Robot Tellers were considered alternative rock, so Sofia was surprised to see people well over middle aged as well as some parents who had brought along their pre-teen children.

"Their music spans generations," Bea told her excitedly as she led Sofia and Travis deep into the front and center of the audience. With Bea's height challenges it was understandable that she wanted to be as close to the front as possible. Standing room only and it was packed. The anticipation in the audience was palpable. A few people were wearing T-shirts with The Robot Tellers emblazoned across the front. Sofia saw at least one T-shirt with Ian's paint splashed image, fist in the air holding a microphone and tongue sticking out aggressively like someone doing the Haka dance.

Dressed in a pair of skinny jeans that accentuated her curves, Sofia had opted out of high heels for the night. Thankfully. She had worn a pair of brown leather boots that went nicely with her peach toned button up tank top and off-white jean jacket. This was about as casual as she could dress, but it would do for a low-key rock concert.

The thing was, she didn't feel low key.

Sofia took a sip of the beer Travis brought her after he stood in a long line at the bar in the back. It did nothing to settle her restlessness. She wasn't the only one. The chatter around her ranged from good-natured drunken banter to gleeful fans getting pumped to see The Robot Tellers.

Was it really possible Ian was this well known? This well liked by so many?

The stage was set up with drums, microphones, electric guitars on stands, and various speakers piled on top of each other on each side. The house lights were on, but when a set of blue spotlights spilled illumination in great cone shapes from the ceiling onto the stage, shouts and screams of encourage-ment arose from the audience. The house lights dimmed.

Sofia thought about Ian's performance at Tawnyetta and Michael's wedding, which she'd witnessed and enjoyed immensely. If the crowd was any indication, he certainly had come a long way from that night. Of course, that had been well over a year ago and this was in an actual venue made for concerts. Not a fancy ballroom in a medieval castle. This was a real rock concert.

"It's going to be so fun," Bea said. She almost had to shout for Sofia to hear her over the whoops and hollers of the fans around them. The lights were shifting from blue to red to purple, faster and faster, whipping up the crowd.

"The Tellers!" A man just behind them shouted into the air. Several fans whistled their appreciation.

A low rumble came from the speakers. The crowd erupted into screams, lifting their arms into the air and pumping their hands up and down. Sofia looked at Travis with wide eyes. She had not been expecting this at all.

The house lights went off. The rumbling stopped. The

pulsing lights on stage froze for an instant...then went totally black, leaving only a few pin points of green and red lights where cords were plugged into speakers. The audience screamed even louder, the sound ringing in Sofia's ears.

A single tone sounded from the stage and held in the air. White stripes of light fanned down from the ceiling and crossed the stage, revealing the shapes of the band moving to their positions. But only for an instant before they disappeared into darkness again. Sofia recognized Ian's body and a shiver tickled down her neck. The single tone shifted one half note up. A pounding drum started. The purple lights blinked on and off with each beat. The audience went completely bonkers.

Just when Sofia thought the anticipation had reached a breaking point, a white spot light shot on at the back of the stage, backlighting Ian and the band.

He raised his hand into the air and shouted into the microphone, "Louder!"

The crowd's reaction was instant and deafening. Before Sofia could wrap her mind around the fact that this man on stage was the same one who had showed up on her doorstep under the guise of returning her sweater, the song began and she, along with the rest of the crowd, was lost in the experience.

The first song was fast and loud. As was the second. Ian alternately grabbed the mic with both hands to sing into it then taking control of his guitar and joining the second guitarist and bass guitarist in playing the all consuming danceable music. The light show was amazing, flashing and strobing, dark and moody one moment, blindingly bright the next, it added to the intensity of each song. Swept away by the sound of it all, Sofia was completely impressed at their music, at Ian's skill as a singer, musician, and all around performer.

She was also thoroughly blown away by the way he looked.

Wearing faded black jeans with a rip in one knee, black lace up boots, a tight black and white bowling shirt, along with his standard silver rings, beaded bracelets, and punked out red hair, on stage apparently was where his style really shone. It wasn't just Ian's look or the music that she was reacting to, however. It was his presence. His confident, smooth, sexy presence that was sending women around her into a frenzy and making her insides feel like electrified jelly.

The third song began. A slower rhythm. A rock ballad.

The lights at the back of the stage grew stronger, illuminating the band and the first section of the audience closest to the stage, of which Sofia, Bea and Travis were part. Ian looked up from adjusting the keys on his guitar and saw them. Recognition ignited his face and he smiled his impossibly engaging smile. He pointed his guitar pick at them.

Bea waved and yelled, "Ian!"

Sofia felt the eyes of everyone nearby turn to them. She froze, not wanting to shout his name, but wanting him to notice her more than anything she'd wanted in a long time.

He stepped up to the mic and pressed his lips against it, "Good to see you." He locked eyes with Sofia and a jolt of energy shot through her heart into her stomach when he said, "Glad you could make it." He turned around and spoke to the bass guitarist who gave Sofia a nod and lifted a finger in greeting. Ian leaned back into the mic and kind of chuckled. He shook his head at whatever he'd been laughing at then ran his hand through his spiked up hair. "Now I'm nervous," he confessed quietly.

The crowd screamed.

Sofia's heart melted just a little bit.

The other guitarist played a surprisingly delicate intro, the drummer started a light beat, and Ian sang the next song. It was a ballad, and it was beautiful.

Follow me, follow me,
I'm chasing the sun,
Finding the melody,
Finding the one.
You're flying high, babe.
Take me to the sky.
Tonight's the night, babe,
Tonight is goodbye.

When did you learn to hate me?
Who told you what to say?
I know nothing's forever,
Don't let it be this way...

When the concert was over, they were bustled backstage by a tall, lanky man with dark skin, kind brown eyes, a long unkempt beard, and a black T-shirt with the word 'STAFF' emblazoned on the back. Forced to walk single file while following him, Bea took the lead, followed by Sofia with Travis last. Bea talked incessantly the whole time, but Sofia couldn't hear what she was saying. The music was still running through her mind and her body, and every sight and sound around her was muffled in comparison.

Sofia's senses were awake, alive with the electrical performance Ian had just given and vibrating with her own private reaction. Logically she knew he was an entertainer, a lead singer, used to the love and adoration of a crowd and expected to put on a good show. But buried under all of this logic was a sensation Sofia didn't want to name. Though she knew he'd been putting on a concert for every person in this room, of which there were probably nearly a thousand, Sofia felt as if he had meant it all for her.

"Don't be ridiculous," she muttered under her breath. They had been on one date. One failed date, she might add.

Failed because she had cut it short and cut him off, denied any desire to see him again. Another thought flashed through her mind. Had she made a mistake?

They were shown behind a heavy black curtain to a beat up door at the left of the stage. The door, too, was black. Though the paint job was at least a decade old and had been embellished by various stickers over the years. As they ducked through the door and entered backstage Sofia was taken back to high school when Luna convinced her it would be fun to help stage manage their production of Little Shop of Horrors. Angie had played Audrey and Thomas had played the bad guy, the abusive dentist. They had both been pretty good as Sofia recalled.

This backstage was a labyrinth of high ceilinged halls dotted with nondescript doors. All closed. Dimly lit and lined with rock band posters, the floors were plain cement and the entire place was begging for a coat of fresh paint, not to mention more light fixtures. Unlike Sofia's high school theater, this backstage felt better used. It also smelled like stale beer and full ashtrays.

They came upon a door with no special markings where their bearded guide stopped. "Here you are, then," he said, pushing the door open and holding it so they could enter.

Inside the room four people, three men and a woman, lounged in varying degrees of exhaustion on two outdated, but comfortable looking, couches. A portable card table with two open bags of potato chips and two six packs of Stella Artois, both with cans missing, sat alone on the far wall. All eyes turned towards them as they entered and Sofia immediately recognized the three men as the other members of The Robot Tellers.

The bass player, the one who had pinkie waved at her from the stage, nodded at them in greeting. He was a tall black man who wore a folded bandana like a sweatband around his head, making the rest of his naturally curly hair stick up in a high Afro.

"You're Ian's friends?" he asked.

"Yes," Bea answered for all of them. "Is he here?"

The bass player unfolded from the couch as he spoke, "Yeah, he went looking for you I think." He looked directly at Sofia and she felt the woman on the couch sizing her up. "I'm Hugh," the bass player stuck out his hand to shake Travis' and then her and Bea's. "Come in, he'll be back when he doesn't find you."

The two other men were the lead guitarist and drummer, Danny and Charlie, respectively. They both had bushy blonde hair, wiry frames, and looked like they were in need of a home cooked meal. Charlie was much bigger than Danny, who was a man of diminutive size, but their voices sounded alike and Sofia wondered if they were related in some way. The woman was introduced as Emery, just Emery. No musical title or back-stage job, like 'manager' or 'van driver', or anything like that. She was late twenties, small with a platinum blonde pixie cut that she had done up with product so it stuck out in all direc-tions. Tan, fit, with big, blue eyes and full lips coated thick with pale pink lipstick, Emery wore a tight pink crocheted tank top dress that barely covered her assets. Her purse was white patent leather with a strap made to look like a giant golden chain. The chain was positioned between her breasts and its pull made their size and shape, and the fact that she wasn't wearing a bra, even more noticeable.

Groupie. This was the first word that came to Sofia's mind when Hugh introduced them. Emery's smug smile did nothing to change that impression.

"And you are, who, exactly?" Emery asked. Sofia had not been long in London, but she thought she recognized a certain lower class edge to Emery's accent. Maybe that was being too harsh.

Sofia raised one eyebrow and started to speak, but the door opened, interrupting her before she had a chance.

"Hullo! There you are!" Ian said as he joined them.

Sofia was unprepared to see him up close and personal. A burst of emotion swelled up inside of her, threatening to come out in the form of a fit of giggles or, even worse, an embarrassing gush of happiness. Sofia squelched those possibilities by slamming her lips together and holding them tight, which may or may not have made her look bizarre. She had no choice. She could not allow an overreaction.

Ian, on the other hand, did not hold back his excitement on seeing her—or them, rather. His smile lit up his face and eyes. And she couldn't help but notice that his shirt was completely unbuttoned, showing glimpses of his very defined and tattooed chest and stomach. Add that to what must be a post-show glow after being onstage and he was, in this moment, one of the handsomest men she'd ever seen in her life.

"Oh, Ian, that was marvelous. Really, really, marvelous," Bea squealed and opened her arms for a congratulatory hug. Leave it to Bea to do the gushing.

"Thanks, Bea," Ian leaned down and gave her a warm hug, then shook Travis' hand. "Travis, good to see you." Travis mumbled something about a good show. Then Ian turned his golden cat eyes on her with a sensual appreciation that increased her heart rate. "Sofia, you look beautiful."

Her resolve to keep her mouth clamped shut and remain calm and collected began to unravel. Her mind raced for something to say. Something cool, intelligent, memorable.

"Thanks," she blurted out like she was in junior high and Ian was Mitchel Johnson, her childhood crush.

Amusement filled his eyes, like he found her charming, not like he was laughing at her discomfort. He glanced around the room and noticed Emery sitting like a sexy pink pillow on the couch. The amusement drained away and something closer to confusion replaced it.

"Oh, you're here," he said, the emphasis on *you're*. He shot a look at Hugh who was standing uncomfortably by the snack and beer table. He gave Ian a barely perceptible shrug of apology.

"Yes," Emery stood up and Sofia noticed her hot pink stilettos for the first time. Emery put all of her weight on one foot and stuck the opposite hip out, cocking her head at Ian. "*I'm* here."

Chapter Eleven

To say Emery was a groupie would be incorrect. To say she was Ian's girlfriend would also be incorrect. To say she was something undefined that floated in between those two labels would be spot on.

In all truth, Sofia didn't want to say any of those things. She didn't want to think about Emery, because when she did she felt a stinging sensation of jealousy slither up her spine. Not that she had any claims on Ian. And even if she did, jealousy would only poison whatever relationship they did have. But she wasn't in a relationship with Ian. A fact she had to repeatedly remind herself during the rest of the evening.

In actions and words, Ian came across as very interested in Sofia romantically. He also came across as charming, witty, and flirtatious with her...and with Emery...and even with Bea. Not that she honestly believed he was hitting on Bea, nothing he did went that far. She just noticed that he was a fun loving guy in general, with a lot of people. And Sofia was just one of them. She wasn't exactly sure how she felt about that.

Sofia didn't have much time to think about any of it

before she was pulled along to an after-party at The Sneezing Pigeon, ironically. There she fought a silent battle with her emotions. On one hand, she couldn't deny that she was attracted to Ian. Intensely. Watching him on stage she had been so impressed with his talent and his energy. Maybe even interested enough to reconsider going on a second date. On the other hand, she couldn't help but notice his lifestyle wasn't what she considered stable. It wasn't relatable to her experience. Since they'd gotten to the pub, he spent much of his time with her, he also spent time with fans and other musicians. It seemed that there were a lot of people clamoring for his attention. He even spent a few minutes with Emery in a rather intense conversation at a corner table.

"They're not going out, if that's what you're thinking," Bea informed her with a sideways comment as they watched Emery slide her hand up Ian's arm possessively.

Sofia pushed the toe of her foot along a line on the hardwood floor, staring at it as she did, trying to look nonchalant. "Who?"

Bea gave her a little eye roll. "Ian, silly. That's what you're thinking isn't it? That Emery is his girlfriend?"

Sofia acted casually surprised and pretended to look for Emery and Ian, as if she didn't know where they were in the crowd. "I wasn't thinking anything," she lied.

Bea let out a little sigh of frustration, "Right. Well, just so you know, they were an item until almost two years ago. But Ian told me himself that they broke up and he is not seeing anyone right now."

If that was supposed to make her feel better, it didn't. Knowing that Emery had a history with him gave her a sinking feeling. Even though Ian may have expressed his indifference to Bea, it was obvious to Sofia that Emery was anything but a forgotten ex-girlfriend.

Sofia took a sip of her whiskey sour. After all the ups and

downs of the evening she had felt like having a strong drink. The burning liquor wasn't helping her mood much. In fact, it was making her feel a little sick. Or maybe it was the whole situation that was making her ill. Either way, she really just wanted to go home. She had kept her word and come to the concert. There was nothing more for her here. She would be better off getting some rest so she could tackle her work projects on Monday with all of her energy.

So, when Ian was fully distracted and not looking in her direction, Sofia said her goodbyes to Bea and Travis.

"Would you like us to walk you home?" Travis offered.

"Not necessary," Sofia said. "I'll get a cab. I'm not too far from here. Thank you, though."

Travis looked a little disheartened. His introverted self probably wouldn't mind going home either.

"You don't want to say goodbye to Ian?" Bea asked hopefully.

"Tell him goodbye from me, and thank him for inviting me to the concert, I had a great time," she responded. Then she made her escape.

By the next afternoon Sofia felt much better. With some distance between her and Ian's intense physical presence, she was able to put their entire interaction into perspective. While it was a pleasant diversion, dating a rock star was definitely not part of her grand life plan. There was no reason to pursue such an ill-advised match in her opinion.

She spent all day reading her pile of books, finishing her ironing, and catching up on emails and social media with her friends and family back home. Mid-afternoon she left to go for a little walk to get some fresh air. She thought she might pop by the funny gingerbread candy store and pick up some more treats. Luna was supposed to call her sometime today, so Sofia left her phone volume up as she strolled to the candy store.

"So, you're back," the shop lady said brightly as Sofia

stepped inside to the sound of tinkling bells ringing above the door.

"I am," she answered. "I'm addicted to Pear Drops!"

"Aren't we all?"

Just as she was about to put in her order, Sofia's cell rang loudly from deep in her purse.

"Excuse me," she said and stepped back out the door politely. When she got hold of her phone it was on the third ring, but instead of Luna's picture popping up on the screen, it was the selfie she had taken with Ian on the London Eye. Unfortunately, she had attached it to his phone number in her phone in a moment of weakness. Seeing it pop back up like this sent a flurry of butterflies through her. Ian was calling.

Her finger hovered over the screen for a long moment as she decided what to do. Then, when she was about to answer it, the phone stopped ringing. It had gone to voicemail. Standing in the middle of the sidewalk Sofia stared at the now blank screen where she and Ian's selfie had just glowed, happy and fun. A twinge of disappointment quivered in her heart, but she shook it off. Probably for the best.

She turned back into the candy shop and put on a bright smile for the nice shop lady, who introduced herself as Lottie.

"My Mum used to buy us five pence of Pear Drops when we went on picnics," Lottie explained as she plunged a shiny contoured scooper into a bulbous glass jar filled with the pale pink and yellow candies.

"I'll want a few more than five pence worth I think," Sofia said, much to Lottie's amusement.

She left the store with a small brown bag half full of her newest favorite treat. 100 grams worth. She was still not used to counting everything in grams, but she had more than enough in her little bag.

Instead of turning right and heading back to her flat, Sofia turned left toward the Thames. It was a pleasant afternoon.

Overcast and not too hot, she thought a walk along the river would be good to clear her head. Clear her head from what, exactly? She couldn't, or didn't want to, put her finger on it, but Sofia felt restless. Dissatisfied.

She popped a Pear Drop in her mouth to enjoy as she walked. Once on the tree lined path, she went the opposite direction of the way she normally took to King's College. It was Sunday and she didn't want to think too much about work if she could help it. The path was busy, but not uncomfortably so. Bicyclists rang little bells to warn pedestrians on foot that they were approaching. Couples walked hand in hand. Dogs led their owners on leashes. A huge barge passed slowly on the wide river along with other smaller vessels, some of which looked like luxury passenger boats.

After about 20 minutes of walking, Sofia found an unoccupied bench and sat down to look out over the water. She had grown up in Denver, Colorado, which had a lot to offer as far as outdoor experiences. Something Denver did not have, however, were large bodies of water like oceans and rivers. Not rivers like the Thames anyway. She took a deep breath of the damp air. Seagulls, who apparently lived everywhere in the world, called out in the distance and she watched them fly and dip down over the water. It was all very nice. Very, very nice. Really, really, *really* nice.

She sighed. What was her problem? Sofia popped another Pear Drop into her mouth. She knew what the problem was, but she was angry that it was a problem at all. It was her phone. Her stupid 'always connected to the world can't have a day to herself' cell phone. That ridiculously adorable picture of her and Ian on The London Eye. Glancing up she could see the Eye in the distance. It was over 450 feet high and twirled around like a stupid giant Ferris wheel, of course she could see it. Nothing about her date with Ian would be ignored.

She sighed again, frustrated at her weakness.

While she'd been chatting with Lottie and trying to enjoy her Sunday off she had felt her phone buzz in her purse, letting her know that she had a voicemail. Since that moment the thought of Ian leaving a voicemail had pricked at the back of her mind like a fly trapped in a window trying to get to the outside. Annoying. Relentless. Futile.

What could he possibly have said in a voicemail? They had no plans. She had not agreed to see him again. Surely Bea and Travis would respect her wishes and not encourage him in pursuing her anymore. She leaned back against the bench and focused hard on relaxing. In her peripheral vision she could see the giant, slow moving cantilever that was the London Eye. Sofia growled under her breath. She would listen to his message.

Reaching for her purse she heard her phone erupt into vibration and ringtone. He was calling again.

With exasperation she shoved her hand in her purse and yanked out her phone. The picture showing on the screen was not the offending ginger haired rock star. It was Luna.

"Luna!" Sofia answered with relief and a twinge of disappointment she tried to cover up.

"Hi cousin, how are you?" Luna's voice, sweet and familiar.

"Oh, you know..." Sofia started to speak when without any warning at all her voice trembled and she couldn't continue without crying.

"What's the matter?" Luna asked. If she couldn't hear Sofia struggling to speak through tears, she most certainly sensed it. They were close. Also, Luna was highly intuitive.

"Nothing, not really..." Sofia managed.

"Something's the matter," Luna pressed.

"I'm just..." Sofia searched for an excuse Luna would accept. She didn't want her to think she was blubbering about some man. "I think I'm homesick," she sniffled. That wasn't exactly untrue.

"Oh, honey," Luna cooed.

"I think I've just been so busy, you know? And now that I have a little down time...I'm missing home," Sofia explained, pleased that she was able to say it without breaking down in public.

Luna understood, asked questions, and listened patiently as Sofia told her about her flat, her job, Bea and Travis, and purposefully excluded Ian.

At a lull in the conversation, Luna asked, "What about the cute guy?"

Sofia swallowed. "What cute guy?

"The guy in the picture! Thomas sent it to everyone," Luna explained. "So who is it? Bridget thinks it's the rock star from London."

Sofia deflated slightly. She wasn't going to be able to keep up her nonchalance with Luna. Luna sensed every emotion someone had almost before they had it.

"I wouldn't exactly call him a rock star," Sofia said. On the other side of the world, Luna squealed. "It's nothing. He's nobody," Sofia tried to sound convincing.

"He didn't look like nothing," Luna giggled.

"He just showed me around the city a little bit. No big deal."

"Hmm..."

Sofia could tell Luna didn't quite believe her. "He's not really my type, cuz," she said, trying to blow the whole thing off.

"That's exactly why I was excited for you!"

"There's nothing to be excited about. Not with him anyway."

"Okay," Luna paused. "You look really good in that picture," she added. "Happy."

Sofia closed her eyes and pinched the bridge of her nose, then changed the subject.

Chapter Twelve

nother week of work flew by and before Sofia could blink, Tawnyetta and Michael were back in London on more fundraiser errands. It seemed to her that they could conduct more of these meetings on a conference call or over Skype to avoid making the trip all the way to London from the Highlands every other weekend. But maybe they liked the traveling.

"You two certainly are busy with this event," Sofia commented as they approached the car and driver Michael had rented to take them around for the day. The two shared a look and Sofia narrowed her eyes at them suspiciously. "What?"

"I'll tell you in the car," Tawnyetta promised. She seemed agitated, excited about something. So did Michael.

"So what's going on?" Sofia pressed once they were settled in their seats and Michael had given the address of their destination to the driver. "Where are we going?"

"We're making one wee stop on our way to Bea and Travis' for dinner," Michael explained. "But that's not the big news."

Sofia looked from him to Tawnyetta and back again. They

were both beaming and she couldn't imagine what in the world was making them so giddy.

"I'm pregnant," Tawnyetta exclaimed, throwing her hands out in celebration.

It took a few moments for her friend's words to sink in. Sofia was stunned. This had not been on her radar at all.

"What?!" she exclaimed.

Michael threw his arm over Tawnyetta's shoulders and pulled her to him, kissing her temple. Tawnyetta flushed prettily, still beaming from her news and nodded emphatically.

"I know! We weren't expecting...to be expecting!" Tawnyetta laughed.

"Congratulations!" Sofia broke free of her surprise and leaned across the car seat to hug them both. "Oh my God! This is huge!"

"I know, we have been trying to break the news to everyone. My parents are on a weekend trip to their cabin and don't have cell service. So we haven't been able to reach them yet," Tawnyetta chatted happily. Michael watched her with pride and joy. Their love for each other and their excitement over this baby was obvious.

"How far along are you?"

"Twelve weeks."

Sofia bubbled with questions, but they got all jumbled together. The happy news was making her grin from ear to ear. "I can't even think what to ask you, but I want to know everything!"

"Our wee one is due April 28th," Michael offered.

Sofia put her hand on Michael's knee. "You, sir, are adorable." This made Tawnyetta laugh and Sofia turned her attention to her next. "Have you told everyone?" By 'everyone' she meant the other besties; Bridget, Luna, Angie and Thomas.

"Not yet, although Bridget suspects something. We were

video chatting when I had pretty bad morning sickness. And you know Bridget, she picks up on anything to do with engagements, weddings or babies, and jumps to conclusions."

"But she would be right about this one," Sofia said.

Tawnyetta nodded, "Yes, I just don't want my parents to hear about it from anyone but us. And once Bridget knows for sure, who knows what will happen."

Sofia understood. Then a thought struck her, "So I'm the first one to know?"

Tawnyetta smiled and nodded.

With that they were lost in conversation about pregnancy and babies and everything that entails. Sofia and Tawnyetta kept chattering and giggling in the car, in the elevator, all the way up to the door where Michael stopped and knocked.

"What is this place?" Sofia finally thought to ask.

"Michael's friend, you know him–" Tawnyetta's explanation was cut short by the door opening.

Sofia's brain raced ahead of what Tawnyetta was saying and she knew with a sudden rush of surprise, even before seeing him, that it was Ian's flat. Sure enough, he pulled the door wide open and smiled at them. She sucked in a breath before she could stop herself and Tawnyetta gave her a sideways glance.

"Hullo," he greeted them.

Sofia's emotions were everywhere. She'd been so wrapped up in Tawnyetta's big news she hadn't given one thought to anything else. And now, as Ian stood there grinning, the familiar thrill of being in his presence returned.

He wore an olive green dress shirt that was untucked and rolled up at the sleeves. The color suited him, especially his golden eyes that were dancing at her with an intimacy she knew the others did not see.

"Ian, how've you been?" Michael grabbed Ian's hand and they pulled in for a brief man hug.

"Good, good," Ian answered. He stepped back and ushered them inside, "Come in."

Tawnyetta stopped and gave him a hug. Then it was Sofia's turn. Still tongue tied and not sure how to act, she paused in front of him, the scent of his cologne tickling her nose. Ian looked down at her and paused for a mere millisecond, searching her eyes with his. In that brief moment she saw amusement, embarrassment and attraction in his eyes, and felt her own convey the same to him.

With a hint of a nervous swallow, he said, "Hullo, Sofia."

"Hello," she answered. She let her eyes linger on his, enjoying the secrecy they shared. Then she dropped her gaze and followed Tawnyetta and Michael into the living room.

Ian's flat was a loft. High-ceilings with exposed beams, floor to ceiling windows on the outside wall, and modern, if slightly used, furniture throughout.

"This is a wee bit nicer than your last place," Michael said as he looked around the room.

Ian laughed in agreement, "You're right about that."

They sat on a low black sectional sofa while Ian got them drinks. Stella in bottles for Michael and Sofia, and a sparkling water for Tawnyetta. Three tall narrow abstract paintings hung on the wall behind the sofa. Black, blue, red, green and yellow paint splattered in different patterns on each. In the corner of the room next to the windows were five different guitars placed on stands, two acoustic and three electric. There was also a keyboard, a microphone on a mic-stand, and two tall stools.

"Sure you don't want anything stronger?" Ian asked Tawnyetta. "I've got mixers."

"No, thank you..." Tawnyetta gave Michael a look full of meaning.

Michael cleared his throat and said, "Actually, Ian, there's a reason Tawnyetta can't drink." An unabashed look of pride came over his face. "She's expecting."

For a moment Sofia could tell Ian was processing what he'd just heard. He looked dumbly at Michael, then at Tawnyetta, then at her for verification. Sofia nodded almost imperceptibly at him.

"What's this?" Ian let out a shocked laugh. Michael's eyes twinkled with pride. Tawnyetta blushed and Sofia thought she had never looked lovelier. "That's fantastic news, isn't it? Congratulations!"

Ian's reaction charmed Sofia. He was boyishly shy when speaking to Tawnyetta and overwhelmingly enthusiastic with Michael. He sat down next to Sofia while they chatted about the big news and was so comfortable that she felt like they were a couple. As if Tawnyetta and Michael had popped over to their house to make the announcement. Sofia liked that feeling and found it difficult to ignore Ian's lean frame sitting next to hers.

Tawnyetta's cell phone buzzed in her purse. She checked it and said, "It's my Mom."

Michael stood up, "We should talk to her together." He looked at Ian, "Do you have another room we could step into for a moment?"

Ian showed them through a door that she presumed led to his bedroom. Sofia sipped her drink and let her eyes wander around the tastefully decorated living room. She wondered what his bedroom looked like.

"So," he said as Ian closed the door and turned to her with a mischievous smile. "Alone at last." He took three long steps and hopped over the edge of the sofa, landing in a seated position next to her. Close, but not touching. She yelped in surprise then giggled. Ian threw his arm on the back of the sofa and raised one eyebrow at her. "I take it my blistering good looks, natural charm, and rock star status has not impressed you."

She acted shocked. "Why would you say that?"

He grimaced and sucked air through his teeth. "I did give you a ring, and you didn't answer, and you didn't ring me back."

"Oh, that," she arched her brows at him. "I guess I was busy."

He chuckled, looking across the room as if thinking of something clever to say. Sofia found her gaze drifting across his jaw to the tattoo on his neck, which flexed as he turned back to face her. For a long moment he looked into her eyes and the air seemed to sparkle between them. Then he made a decision and solidified it with a quick nod to himself. "Friends, then?" he asked.

Sofia suddenly realized she'd been leaning into him and their shoulders were touching. She pulled away and cleared her throat so she could speak, "I'm afraid so."

Ian let out a sigh by puffing up his cheeks and blowing the air out through pursed lips. "All right, then. If you insist. Friends it is."

A pang of disappointment moved through her, but it was for the best. She was sure of it.

"This is a really nice flat," she tried to change the subject.

"Thank you," he said, taking a swig of his beer.

As he moved his arm muscles flexed. He held the beer bottle in his hand, turning it and running his finger along the label. Her eyes were drawn to his Beatles tattoo and there was a tingle in her fingertips, urging her to touch it, to touch him. Sofia stood up. Ian's eyes followed her.

"These are all yours?" She moved to the guitars in the corner and pretended to study them intently. Stupid question, but all she could think of in the moment.

He followed her and stood at her elbow before answering, "Yes, every one."

"They're really beautiful," she said, admiring the graceful lines of each guitar.

"Do you play?"

"Oh, no," she scoffed at the idea. "I never had time for music lessons." The comment came out more wistfully than she had meant it to. She glanced at Ian who was watching her evenly.

"Lessons..." he lifted a white electric guitar with a dark red stripe through the middle of it off of its stand. "Who's had lessons?" She giggled. "I'll show you," he offered. He placed his beer on the floor next to the wall and did the same with hers. "Are you right handed?" he asked. She nodded and he flipped the guitar around so she could take hold of it.

"Oh," she said as she took it. "It's heavy."

"A bit," Ian agreed as he lifted the strap over her head and around her shoulders. She adjusted the guitar in her arms until it was comfortable. "Good?" he asked.

"Yes, I guess," she said. "Is it going to be loud?"

Ian squatted down and fiddled with the plugs in a strip on the floor. "Oh, yes," he said. "Absolutely."

She wrapped her hand around the neck of the guitar and ran a pale pink fingernail down one of the strings, which was made of steel. News to her. She'd never even taken a close look at an electric guitar.

"Here we are," Ian stood up, digging a guitar pick out of his jeans pocket and handing it to her. He positioned himself behind her and to the right. "Now, how about a power chord?"

Sofia laughed, "Sure."

Ian took hold of her index finger and gently showed her how to press down on all but the top string. He hovered over her shoulder and gave her instructions, the sound of his voice and his breath on her neck giving her goose bumps.

"Now, give the top string a pluck with your pick," he told her.

She did. A low tone reverberated out of the amplifiers and she felt a faint buzz in her fingers and hands.

"Oh!" Sofia said in surprise. Turning her face toward Ian standing behind her, she laughed. "That sounds pretty good!"

"Doesn't it?" Ian leaned in closer and looked over the neck of the guitar, placing his hand over hers and rearranging her fingers for another chord. "Now do it again," he instructed.

She did. Another note reverberated through the room. Sofia giggled. Giddiness came over her and try as she might she could not keep it under control. The feel of the guitar in her hands, the notes that actually sounded good humming through the room, and Ian standing a hair's breath away from her, his deep, smooth voice speaking right into her ear, was affecting her mood. She was having a hard time remembering that she only wanted to be friends.

As the night wore on Sofia tried to maintain as platonic a connection to Ian as possible. And failed miserably.

Chapter Thirteen

Bea had really outdone herself. Seafood risotto, cold broccoli salad, fresh Italian bread, white wine, and chocolate clementine torte for dessert. Delicious food, a beautiful table set with fresh flowers and candles, funky jazz playing softly in the background, everything was over the top well done.

"Fantastic," Michael declared after savoring his first bite of the torte and grunting with pleasure.

Bea blushed furiously then giggled into her napkin. They had all complimented her for the meal throughout dinner, but she seemed to find Michael's praise especially flustering.

"It's Jamie's...Jamie Oliver's," she explained. "I wanted to make something really special for tonight, you see. So I pulled out my handy copy of *Jamie Cooks Italy*." She smiled brightly at Michael.

"Well done. This is simply delicious," Michael responded, lifting another bite of torte on his fork towards her in a toast before popping it into his mouth.

A thought occurred to Bea and she held up her hand and shook it. "Not that, actually. The torte recipe came from his

Friday Night Feast's book. But I thought it would be perfect for tonight. And I didn't even know about the big news!" She giggled again. "Just a lucky guess I suppose. A torte to celebrate the new baby! I'm so happy for you both."

Travis gave his wife a funny look, but she didn't respond. She didn't even look at him, just kept her eyes on Michael as words continued to spill out of her mouth. Sofia glanced at Tawnyetta, who watched Bea with calm amusement.

"I got the bread from our local bakery. A lovely older couple run it. They are so kind and helpful. I told them we were having a Lord and Lady for supper tonight and they gave me their best loaf." Bea giggled again then saw her husband's face and swallowed hard.

Travis looked abashed. He cleared his throat in what appeared to be an attempt to stem the flow of comments coming from his bride. But when he opened his mouth, Bea interrupted him.

"Of course, the broccoli salad is an old standby. I found that recipe years ago in *The Naked Chef.*" Bea's hands flew to cover her mouth as she gasped. "I just said 'naked' in front of a Lord!" She giggled maniacally into her hands.

Travis jerked out of his chair, clattering his plate and silverware in his hurry. "Come on, darling. I'll help you clear the table."

Sofia looked at Ian who was smiling as he chewed a bite of torte and watched Bea's antics. Michael was absorbed in his own dessert, leaving Sofia and Tawnyetta to share a sympathetic smile for their friend.

"She's a little flustered, I think," Sofia offered.

Tawnyetta nodded, looking at her husband who appeared to be the main cause of Bea's nervousness. "Sometimes I'm surprised at how people react to the title 'Lord'."

Michael swallowed his torte and took a sip of his after dinner coffee. He shook his head and corrected her, "It's pronounced *Laird*." He winked at Tawnyetta and she pushed on his arm in mock reproach.

"Aw, she's just a little struck," Ian said. Having just finished his dessert, he leaned back in his chair, musing, "She's just a proper English girl, that's all. Maybe American girls don't get tongue tied around royalty?" He was talking to all of them, but looking at Sofia, waiting for her reaction.

She frowned and said, "I don't like to categorize people." Ian grinned.

"We're not royalty," Tawnyetta corrected. "Besides, we're friends! She was at our wedding for goodness sake."

Sofia heard a note of concern in her voice. If Tawnyetta was one thing, it was down to earth. She was probably extremely uncomfortable knowing that Bea was nervous to have her or Michael in her home.

"I wouldn't worry about it," Ian said. "Travis will talk her through it and she'll be right as rain when she comes back." Tawnyetta was still bothered. "How about I create a distraction when they get back? You know, get her mind off of it," Ian offered.

They all turned to him. Tawnyetta and Michael from across the table, Sofia from the chair next to him. They'd been seated like they were a couple at the dinner table and Ian had freely nudged her and made quiet comments to her throughout the evening. Despite everything she'd decided about him, Sofia had liked it. With a questioning look, he seemed to be specifically asking her permission about this idea.

"What kind of distraction?" Michael asked, looking at Ian with skepticism.

"I don't know..." They all thought for a long moment. Then Ian hit the table with his palm. Dishes rattled. "I'll toast the baby!"

Before they had time to consider this option, Travis and Bea came back in the room. Travis cleared his throat, but appeared to be struggling to find words. Bea averted her eyes bashfully and Sofia's heart went out to her. There was a long, uncomfortable pause which was making the whole situation much more awkward than it warranted. Sofia couldn't stand it anymore. Under the table she found Ian's leg with her foot and gave him a soft kick. He sprang into action.

"Brilliant! You're back," Ian exclaimed, standing up. He gestured for Travis and Bea to sit down while he picked up the wine bottle. "I'd like to take this opportunity to make a toast to the newest member of the MacBrody clan...baby Mac." Everyone chuckled.

Relieved to get out of the spotlight, Travis and Bea sat down as Ian distributed a splash of wine in everyone's glass except Tawnyetta's, who was drinking lemonade. Sofia watched Ian expertly handle the mood of the table and thought about his presence on stage when he was performing. He definitely had a way about him. He could take over a room.

"First," Ian stood up straight and addressed Travis and Bea. "A special thanks for yet another delicious homemade meal here at Chez Prescott." Ian bowed politely at them and the table echoed his praise. Bea blushed, happily this time. Ian turned to Michael and Tawnyetta. "And now, to the subject of the *wee bairn*." Again, they all chuckled. Tawnyetta's cheeks turned pink. "Michael, when this beautiful woman agreed to be your bride I thought you must be the luckiest man on the face of the earth." Michael nodded at this and took Tawnyetta's hand as they listened. "But when you told us this evening that you were going to be a father, that you both were going to be parents," Ian's voice slipped a little.

From where Sofia sat next to him she could see the reflection of candlelight in his eyes, which were wet with emotion. She realized this wasn't just a show put on solely to benefit

Bea's feelings. A warm tingle filled her as she watched and listened.

Ian cleared his throat and continued, "When you made the announcement I knew that this was something even bigger, even better. You have been blessed with the task of bringing another soul into the world." Tears welled up in Sofia's eyes unexpectedly. She brushed them aside. "And I congratulate you both, we all do." Ian raised his glass toward the happy couple and they all followed suit. "Now, let me see if I can remember..." he wrinkled his brow for a moment, thinking. Then his face broke into that one of a kind brilliant smile. He finished his toast in a perfect Scottish brogue. "May the dreams you hold dearest be those which come true and the kindness you spread keep returning to you."

"So happy for you," Bea exclaimed.

"Here, here!" Travis offered.

"Thank you, my friend," Michael said sincerely.

Sofia caught Tawnyetta's eye and felt the joy and excitement emanating from her friend. For a few moments all six of them were held inside a warm bubble of love.

"And now...a song!" Ian announced.

Settled in the living room on the edge of the couch, Sofia knew there was no escaping the almost electrical buzz between her and Ian. He sat close to her on a wooden chair they'd brought in from the kitchen, a guitar that Travis kept from his college days in his arms. As his attention was fixed on tuning the guitar, Sofia watched him. He hummed quietly to himself, lost in his music. Lean muscles in his forearms and hands flexed as he tested the guitar, he slid his body back and forth slightly on the seat of the chair adjusting his position.

The details of the tattoo on his neck were clear to Sofia from this vantage point, red roses in black chains, and she had to fight the urge to reach out and run her finger along its edges. Without warning, Ian turned to her, his eyes golden and smiling. She caught her breath, embarrassed because she'd been staring, but not able to look away. He gave her a wink and her stomach turned to jelly.

"All right, now," he said to the two married couples seated comfortably just a few feet away. "Let's all just settle down. No pushing or shoving. You'll all be able to hear once I get started."

"Down in front," Travis called out. He snickered hard, his nose turned red on the tip from laughing at his own joke.

Ian widened his eyes and nodded in appreciation. "There you go, Prescott, having a laugh." He strummed the guitar and cleared his throat. "This is something I've been working on."

His fingers plucked on the strings and the music moved through Sofia's body. Soft tremors. Gentle sounds. Ian closed his eyes as he played moving his body back and forth ever so slightly to the rhythm. He turned his head away from all of them and cleared his throat. She couldn't tell for sure, but she thought maybe he was nervous. Playing in this close proximity without the benefit of a band or microphone or light show was far more intimate. He was far more vulnerable here.

Sofia found herself wanting to be closer to the sound. Closer to him. Her insides were swirling, dancing, losing sight of anything except the sound of his playing and the look on his face. The intro to the song slowed and Ian, still with his eyes closed, took a deep breath and began to sing.

Little one, little one, bring me your heart,
Show me your secrets, show me your scars.
You take me down, you leave me lying there.
You bring me hope then take me to despair.

Shine on me, shine on me, bring me your light.
Take my heart, take my breath, take my life.

Pretty one, pretty one, see what you've done?
Give me your smile, know you're the one.
My eyes are blurred, you are sight to me.
My life is gone when you're not next to me.

Shine on me, shine on me, bring me your light.
Take my heart, take my breath, take my life.

When he was done the notes of his song softly echoed through the small living room. The strength of Ian's singing voice was impressive, but the emotion he poured out when he sang was nothing less than hypnotic. They all sat in silence letting the music and lyrics echo in their souls. Sofia most of all.

In those moments immediately after his song, with his eyes still closed and his face still contorted with emotion, Ian Law owned the room. He also owned Sofia's heart. Her power to resist him fell away like so many petals from a flower. He made her unsteady in her convictions, distracted from her plans, which was how she ended up in a completely new kind of predicament two weeks later when Ian invited her to accompany him on a short trip to one of his scheduled gigs.

Chapter Fourteen

He convinced her to go with him for the weekend. He told her it was the perfect chance for her to get away and see the English countryside. He said she would have fun. And he swore they were going as just friends.

Huge box elder plants that had been pruned for over two centuries into a life size maze flanked them. The deep green, shining leaves were so thick and well shaped they were literally like walls. Even if they had wanted to cheat and break through them to get out of the maze, it would have been impossible. When they started the little adventure for some afternoon entertainment, Sofia anticipated the challenge with excitement. She was good with numbers and puzzles. Surely a life-size maze created centuries ago would not prove to be a problem too big for her to solve.

As she and Ian wandered about, making a left turn here, a right turn there, and backtracking once then twice, Sofia was no longer certain she knew where they were.

"Now don't get nervous," Ian said. He paused and took her by the arms, turning her so they were face-to-face.

"I'm not nervous," Sofia lied. She didn't want to admit defeat because she was lost, and she certainly did not want to admit that she was nervous.

"See that man?" Ian pointed to what looked like a guard tower in the center of the maze. Two stories high with crisp white paint, it was easily seen above the dark green box elders. An old man with a great round belly sat at the very top shaded by a small peaked roof. He wore a bright green jacket and a flopping green hat with a red plume sticking out of the side.

"Yes, I see him," Sofia answered, wondering how she could have missed him when they arrived.

"He's the guide," Ian explained.

"The guide?"

"If we get lost we ask the guide to help us and he'll tell us what direction to go," he told her. "But we are not lost are we? So there's nothing to worry about, is there?" He sounded like he was trying to convince both of them.

"But won't you be late for the party?" She glanced toward the manor house whose second story was visible in the near distance even from inside this maze. It was a beautiful home, like something from one of the hundreds of period films Luna had dragged her to over the years.

They had come to this country estate for the weekend because Ian was singing at a private event. Not a wedding reception, but a birthday party for the daughter of a wealthy Englishman. Sofia had already forgotten the girl's name. Ian had insisted it was no big deal if she came along. There was no band with him for this gig, just him and his guitar.

"Separate rooms," he assured her when they were making the plans. Sofia had felt a pang of regret over that, but she couldn't argue. It had been her request for them to remain platonic.

Wandering through the maze with Ian she found herself

rethinking that decision over and over. He had been so funny and charming on the drive here. She knew he was interested in more than friendship with her when he asked her to go on this weekend. Even if he didn't say so. And she found herself flip-flopping back and forth between wanting to keep him at arm's length and wanting him to pull her closer.

"I've got time before the gig," he reassured her. "It's just me and the ol' guitar, not a big deal."

They came to a 'T' where they could turn right or left, and stopped.

"What do you think? You're the math whiz," he said.

Sofia glanced up at the guard tower. It helped to know that was the center point of the maze. "I don't think we should go right," she said.

"So the only choice we have is left."

"Technically we could also go backward," she corrected.

He turned to look back from where they had come as if taking great pains to ponder her suggestion. When he turned his gaze back her, his eyes smiled, crinkling at the corners.

"I don't like to go backward, I like to face the future head on," he said. "Or...slightly to the left."

She chuckled, "Okay, left it is."

30 minutes later they were still lost.

"The sun is going down," Sofia warned. She was beginning to feel a little claustrophobic. And hot. There was no breeze in this maze.

"It's not going down," Ian reassured her. "It's just that these damnable box elders are so tall and oppressive they don't let the afternoon light in."

They were at another stopping point, having just turned back from another dead end. Or maybe it was the same dead end and they had revisited it for a third time. Sofia was ready to call it quits.

"I think we should admit defeat," she suggested. "Apparently I'm not as good at puzzles as I thought I was."

"Don't say that. We're not defeated. This is just a little more complicated than we thought it would be when we started."

Sofia raised an eyebrow at him, "You're sweating." Parts of the front of his shirt were wet and his hair was damp at the temples.

"Am I?" He wiped his forehead with the back of his arm then looked down at his shirt. "Nothing wrong with working up a frothy sweat during a challenge," he grinned and put his hands on his hips as if he had reached the top of a mountain. "Nothing wrong with going for the ol' brass ring. Using the ol' noggin and getting a workout at the same time. Nothing to be ashamed of in some good old fashioned perspiration!"

Sofia giggled. "*I'm* sweating," she argued lightly.

Ian looked at her in shock. "No, no, no, Luv...you're glowing."

A tingle went across her skin when he called her 'Luv'. She looked down demurely, trying to hide the slight flush in her cheeks. When she lifted her eyes, Ian was still gazing at her and the air between them sparked. He still had his hands on his hips, but no longer in a comical way. His body had relaxed and his eyes were filled with something close to awe.

The longer he looked at her, the more her body tingled. She thought she should say something, but she couldn't, or maybe she didn't want the feeling to stop. Ian stepped closer, his arms dropping as he hooked his thumbs into his front pockets. Sofia sucked in a breath. She knew what was coming. She'd had enough first kisses to know what it felt like to be mesmerized by another person, drawn into them. Her heart beat faster and she waited as Ian moved even closer, studying her face intently as he did.

Inches away, he stopped. Sofia gazed up at him, her mouth parting automatically as if beckoning his lips to hers. His cologne smelled warm and inviting. His eyes searched hers and she felt like she might explode if he didn't touch her.

"God, you're beautiful," Ian said. His voice was husky. His mouth so near hers.

"Oi!" A shout came from above.

They both jumped and looked toward the sky where the voice had originated.

"Oi!" Again. It was the old man. The guard in the tower. "Maze will be closing in 15 minutes. Do you two think you could get a move on?"

Ian chuckled dryly. His head dropped forward and he stared at the ground shaking his head, incredulous. Not only was there a witness to their intimate moment, it had been interrupted and made awkward.

Ian looked up and called out to the guard, "Give us a minute, please."

There was a slight pause, then, "I've got dinner with the wife in 30." The guard's voice was whinier than one might expect from a person with 'guard' in their title.

Sofia giggled.

Ian looked at her with one eye squinted closed as if the sound of the guard's voice hurt his ears. He sighed in mock frustration and, stilling looking at her, called out, "Give us a hint then!"

"Turn around so you're facing the same as the lady. First right, second left, third left, second right and straight on."

Ian's face screwed into comical concentration. He called out to double check, "First right, second left, third left, second right?"

The guard nodded on his perch making the feather in his hat bob up and down. "Then straight on."

Ian turned the direction Sofia was facing and offered her his arm. She took it and as he led her to the first right, he called out to the guard, "Thank you!" Then under his breath, "Perfect timing, by the way."

Sofia laughed out loud.

~

Ian's performance was brilliant. Sofia watched the reaction of the birthday party crowd and knew that they felt drawn to him and his music as much as she always did. The ballroom at this manor house held a few hundred people and all of them that Sofia could see from her vantage point at the side of the small stage thoroughly enjoyed him. Pride swelled in her chest and she couldn't help but feel giddily flattered when he would turn to her and give her a knowing look from the stage.

Afterward, the glowing birthday girl gushed over him. "Aren't you adorable," she flirted. She wasn't a teenager as Sofia had expected, but a full-grown woman, late twenties at least, surrounded by a gaggle of girlfriends.

"Gina stop drooling over your birthday present," one of the friends teased.

The hackles on the back of Sofia's neck bristled. Gina was her name. Now she remembered.

"But he's adorable," Gina argued with a slight slur. She reached out and petted Ian's bicep with a well-manicured hand dripping with expensive jewelry. She had obviously celebrated her birthday with a few drinks before the concert started.

"He's sexy," another friend announced drunkenly to the world. She blinked lashes thick with goopy mascara and tried to focus in on Ian's face before saying sloppily, "You're sexy!"

Ian handled the small group of privileged groupies with ease. He deftly accepted their attempts at compliments while maintaining proper physical distance from them to avoid being groped. He was professional, kind, and good-natured. As she stood waiting and watching him navigate the crowd, she understood logically that nothing about his actions should make her jealous. Yet jealous was exactly how Sofia felt.

"Having fun?" A thin male voice spoke into her ear. She jumped at the sound and turned to find a pale, short man standing too close behind her. He giggled at her reaction and Sofia recoiled from his sour breath in her face. He held a cocktail and used it to point at her. "You the girlfriend?"

"What?" Sofia responded.

The man appeared to be her same age, but already had thinning blonde hair and an odd liquidity to his bulging eyes that she found repulsive. They reminded her of pale frog eyes.

He leaned closer, raised his voice and enunciated as if she were partially deaf and didn't speak English, "Are you the singer's girlfriend?"

Sofia leaned away from him. Honestly, his breath. She shook her head, partly to deny being Ian's girlfriend and partly because she wanted the strange little man to go away. A gale of drunken female laughter rose out of the crowd of groupies, capturing her attention.

"Oh, I see, a groupie then," the man said. "But a shy one!" His shoulders crumpled as he laughed at his own comment.

"Excuse me," Sofia dismissed him without a glance and moved to another section of the room. She supposed she could interrupt Ian's 'fans', but she didn't want to be the jealous girlfriend type. "I'm not his girlfriend, anyway," she muttered to herself.

An insistent finger tapped hard on her shoulder. Sofia turned sharply, annoyed at the weird little man for bothering her again.

But it wasn't the weird little man. It wasn't a man at all. It was Emery.

Blonde, spiky bangs nearly covering one eye while the other eye glared hot at Sofia, Emery stood with one hand on her hip, the other holding an unlit cigarette. Her angry look raked Sofia up and down before she opened her pink slathered lips and asked, "What in the hell are *you* doing here?"

Chapter Fifteen

Sofia was so shocked to see Emery that she couldn't think of a quippy response. All she could do was stare at her in surprise, taken aback not only at her presence, but also at her open hostility. Emery took a quick step towards Sofia, who leaned back a little at the move. Was she going to take a swing at her?

Emery smirked. "Not up for a scuffle over him, then? Not much of a backbone?" Emery scoffed disdainfully then placed the cigarette between her lips where it was immediately smudged with waxy pink lipstick. She lit the end with a faux jewel lighter and took a deep drag while giving Sofia a scathing look. When she spoke again, smoke puffed out of her nostrils and mouth. "Typical American." She blew what remained in her lungs directly into Sofia's face.

Sofia's surprise disappeared. Heat boiled up through her chest and she narrowed her eyes, glaring unflinchingly into Emery's.

"Don't blow your stink in my face," Sofia warned her. Emery's hardened expression flickered. Sofia had dealt with women like this before. They were bullies, thinking that if they acted tough nobody would ever challenge them and they got to walk all over anyone in their path. Well, Sofia certainly wasn't afraid of this chiquita. "What is your problem, exactly?"

"Are you following him or something?" Emery glanced toward Ian and the crowd of drunk groupies.

"I was invited," Sofia retorted. "Not that it's any of your business."

Emery took another drag of her cigarette and eyed Sofia. This time she turned her head slightly when she exhaled so the smoke went sideways. That was an improvement, but she wasn't backing off completely.

"Gina is my friend. That's why it's my business." She looked toward Ian and the birthday girl again, the anger in her eyes temporarily replaced with pain. "That's how he got this gig, you know. Because of me."

No. Sofia did not know that.

She followed Emery's gaze to Ian and his adoring fans. He had just said something amusing, because they all squealed with laughter. Sofia felt sick to her stomach. He looked towards them, noticing Emery next to her for the first time. Sofia turned away from him before she could see his reaction.

"He's going to be famous," Emery said. Still watching him, she hugged her arms in front of her, holding the burning cigarette limply between two fingers. She continued talking, but didn't seem to care if anyone was listening anymore. Her tone was more sad than bitter, "He's so talented. He just reaches into you and rips out your heart, you know?"

Sofia did know.

"He's got oodles of fans. People wearing T-shirts around, talking about him at the clubs. Robot Tellers this, Robot Tellers that," she laughed, but the sound held no joy. Ian was extricating himself from Gina and her crew, intending to join her and Emery. Emery turned back to Sofia in an attempt to look like she didn't care, but her fingers trembled slightly as she took another drag. Sofia saw the raw emotion in her face, a pathetic misery that she recognized as heartbreak. No longer irritated with Emery, she felt sorry for her. "Word of warning," Emery said as she looked Sofia up and down, this time with far less malice. "Woman to woman."

"Okay," Sofia answered cautiously. She sensed that the threatening Emery had collapsed into a more depressed version, but wasn't completely sure.

"Falling in love with a rock star is the pits. You'll always come in second," Emery said, then glanced over to see Ian moving quickly toward them, ready to intercept their conversation. "It's not worth it," she looked sharply into Sofia's eyes before turning on her heels and disappearing into the crowd moments before he arrived.

Their drive back to London was long.

Fury boiled in her core. Ian had drug her along on a weekend full of drunken party girls who panted after him like dogs in heat, not to mention putting her in the crosshairs of his unstable ex-girlfriend. Instead of the fanciful English country weekend she'd been promised, she had spent much of it watching him with his fans, avoiding Emery and the strange pale man who kept trying to talk to her, and generally feeling out of place and angry. She was angry with Ian, but she was also angry with herself. This whole weekend had been a mistake she should have avoided. All she wanted was to get back to her flat and the college. Period.

Ian watched her warily as he steered the tiny, uncomfortable vehicle he called his car around the country lanes. It was an overcast day, but the lush green hills surrounded them, occasionally serving up a small farm or charming cottage. All beauty of the Sunday morning drive was lost on Sofia, however, as she fumed in the passenger seat.

"So, that was fun?" Ian said hopefully.

Sofia glared at him sideways, refusing to look at him directly.

He cleared his throat and tried again, "Lovely day, isn't it?"

Sofia scoffed then pursed her lips together. She had successfully sidestepped getting into an argument with him the night before by retiring early to her room. There was no need to blow up at him now. Soon they would be back in London and she would move on with her life. They weren't dating. An ugly conversation now wouldn't solve anything and there was, in her opinion, absolutely no point in working things out.

They drove for a few more minutes in uncomfortable silence. Not even any music playing in the car. Just the droning buzz of the engine. Ian went along with her silent treatment at first, choosing to drum on the steering wheel, hum to himself, and check out the view through his rocker sunglasses. After a while, however, he began sneaking looks at her. Sofia could see him out of the corner of her eye, but she didn't react, just stared stiffly ahead.

Finally, he couldn't stand it anymore. "You're not talking to me, is that what this is?"

She did not respond.

He sighed. "You don't want to tell me what's wrong?"

"No," she mumbled, then pressed her lips together again.

"Oh! She's alive, ladies and gentlemen! And she hasn't lost the ability to converse!" He made crowd cheering sounds and wiggled his fingers against the steering wheel.

Sofia turned a wicked glare on him. Not amused.

In a fake reporter voice, Ian continued, "She has found her voice, Gerald, but she is definitely not happy. That much should be obvious to our viewers."

"Stop it," she said crisply.

"Are you going to tell me what's wrong?"

She shook her head 'no'.

He sighed again and looked away from her, frustrated. When he spoke, he did so looking straight ahead through the windshield. "If you don't tell me what's wrong then how am I supposed to know?"

"It doesn't matter," she dismissed his logic with a wave of her hand.

This time Ian scoffed. "Of course it matters. I took you on a weekend and you've been insulted...or hurt...or angered by something. What am I supposed to do about it if I don't know what happened?"

"It doesn't matter because the weekend is over."

"How are we going to move on if you won't talk about it?"

"We? There is no 'we', Ian. There is no moving on."

He was surprised and had to search for words to respond. When he didn't find them, he gripped the top of the steering wheel tightly with both hands. The muscles in his forearms flexed.

Sofia was pleased that she'd finally hushed him, but that feeling passed rapidly. What replaced it was a sickening sadness in the pit of her stomach. To her surprise, tears welled up in her eyes and she had to look out of her window to keep Ian from seeing them.

"It was Emery, wasn't it?" he asked grimly.

She swallowed a hot ball of tears at the back of her throat, but still couldn't answer him. She turned her face further away, afraid he would see that she was about to cry.

"I knew it," he said. "She's always doing this."

That was too much. The sadness swelled to anger and Sofia turned on him, tears rolling down her cheeks, "Always doing what? Ruining your latest conquest? I am not an idiot. I have eyes, Ian. I can see that you love the attention of all those women. Don't blame Emery for the fact that you dumped her and broke her heart, ruined her forever. That's your fault. But don't you dare expect me to just go along with your little plan of seduction! I can see when someone is a player and I don't want to have anything to do with it." Sofia's voice rang through the small car and the echo of it hung in the air for a few beats.

"Is that what she told you?"

"She didn't have to tell me *everything*. I could see it on her face!"

Ian was incredulous. "So, what? You're psychic?"

"Don't."

"Don't what?" Now he was getting angry.

"Don't make fun of me," Sofia had stopped crying and wiped the tears off of her cheeks angrily.

He looked to her then to the road then to her again before sighing with frustration. "I'm not making fun of you, Sofia. I'm trying to understand what Emery told you that would make you so upset."

"Why? So you can smooth it over? Tell me that she lied?"

Ian laughed humorlessly, "She did lie! That's what she does."

Sofia blinked at him. She hadn't considered that Emery had been lying. "What did she lie about?"

"For one, she broke up with me. Several times over the years. The last time, by the way, was over a year ago, almost two." The tone of his voice became calmer as he tried to explain, "We were bad together from the beginning. She liked the fact that I was a singer, but she didn't want me to talk to anybody or perform. It was like she was jealous of the crowd." He glanced at Sofia and continued, "The crowd is part of it, you know. I can't do what I do without having fans. That's the harsh truth of it."

Sofia felt ashamed at her insecurity over the drunk

groupies. Then she remembered something else Emery had said, "Did you get this gig because of her?"

"Is that what she told you?"

"Did you?"

He shook his head in disbelief. Then he half-shrugged and admitted, "Technically, I suppose that's true. She was friends with Gina and her family before I knew them." Sofia started to retort, but he interrupted her, "But Emery and I have known each other for a decade. We know the same people. I can't change that."

"I'm not asking you to change anything," Sofia said hotly.

"Okay, okay..." He watched her carefully for a few moments before continuing, "Like I said, though, we were never right from the beginning. I never felt like I do..." He paused and Sofia could see his jaw flexing as he contained what he was about to say. Just when she thought he wasn't going to continue, he spoke. His voice was soft and a little sad and he didn't look at her as he said, "I never wrote songs for her."

Her anger sputtered like a candle about to go out. "What does that mean?"

Ian kept staring out the windshield, steering the car with tense arms, working through what he should say. Finally, he simply said, "You make me want to write songs."

Sofia's anger and hurt washed away in an instant. She knew without a doubt that the song he had sung in the living room the other night had been written for her. Her heart melted and the tears of anger were gone. But instead of leaving love and joy in their place, they only left an empty hole.

Chapter Sixteen

With nowhere else to direct her emotion, Sofia returned to work on Monday morning with furious intent. She went in a little early, the cool of a fall morning brisk on her cheeks. Happy to have something besides Ian to occupy her mind, she set about making a hot cup of tea from the cart and settled in at her small cubby to get some work done before anybody else arrived.

The sound of her computer waking up was comforting. She was happy to dive into the new data they had gathered last week. Reviewing columns and columns of numbers sounded calming. As her computer booted, Sofia leaned back in her chair and sipped her tea. She gazed out the window at the campus waking up and felt her shoulders relaxing. She was in her element again.

A juicy *harrumph* came from the other room. Professor Shipley's office to be exact. Furrowing her brow, Sofia got up to investigate and was surprised to see Professor Shipley sitting behind a pile of books and paperwork in the light of a single desk lamp. He looked up sharply when she peeked into his office.

"Dr. Venegas." It was a statement more than a greeting.

"Good morning, Professor Shipley. I'm sorry, I didn't know anyone was here yet." She felt the need to apologize. He grunted in response and Sofia assumed their conversation was over. That seemed to be how most of their conversations went, she groveled and he grunted. She turned to go back to her desk when he stopped her.

"I have a question for you," he said gruffly.

She turned back and stepped into his office, just barely. "Yes?"

Professor Shipley moved one pile of paperwork off of a large stack and picked up a thick report their research assistant, Henry, had printed out on Friday. He flipped to the end of the report and turned it toward Sofia, dropping it unceremoniously on the edge of his desk.

"What is this?" He pointed heavily at the page that now lay open.

Sofia stepped forward to look at what he was pointing at, leaning over the report as if it was a strange specimen that couldn't be touched. Scanning the document, her initial reaction was confusion. What was the professor indicating with his thick finger?

He harrumphed again, impatiently this time. Sofia glanced up at him. He was peering at her over the tops of his glasses. In his expression was every moment of disappointment she had ever caused her father as a child and her harshest teachers and professors during her education. Sofia's mouth went dry. She looked back to the report and zeroed in on the numbers, her brain racing to find the answer.

Then she saw it. Shining like a beacon off the page, but not a beacon of hope. One of failure.

Sofia tried to swallow so she could speak, but her throat was just as dry as her mouth.

"Do you see it?" Professor Shipley asked. He knew the answer. He could read it on her face.

Sofia nodded, flushing with embarrassment. "Yes," she croaked.

She did see it. A mistake. A big mistake. There was a gap in the numbers. A gap that would obviously skew the final results reported on the last page of the report. A gap that was so apparent it was like someone behind her was shining a flashlight on that exact section of the paper.

How had this happened? She'd reviewed the numbers herself on Friday before she left early for her trip. Henry and Liza had checked them over, too. Sofia felt sick to her stomach. She hadn't shown them to Dr. Clara before leaving them on Professor Shipley's desk. Obviously, that had been a poor decision.

Professor Shipley picked up the report and shoved it at her unceremoniously. Still looking at her over his glasses, his large, liquid eyes fixed on hers, displeased.

"I'm sorry," she managed. "There's obviously missing data."

"Yes, obviously," he responded. As she picked up the worthless report, he continued, "Details, Dr. Venegas." He stretched the word 'doctor' out with something falling just short of contempt. Sofia shrank from his words, but only on the inside. On the outside she stood straight as an arrow and looked him in the eye as he spoke. "Details cannot be brushed aside. They cannot be overlooked. They cannot be missed."

"Yes, sir."

Professor Shipley looked at her sharply, trying to determine if she was sufficiently contrite or if she was being flippant.

"Good morning! I brought breakfast!" Dr. Clara poked her head into the office. Sofia used the distraction of her arrival to duck out of Professor Shipley's office and avoid further reprimands. She hurried to her cubby hole desk and tossed the incorrect report on her desk. Her tea was cold. Skinny raindrops slicked the window. The day outside was turning out to be gloomy, just like everything else in her life.

Later in the afternoon, Sofia's sick stomach had migrated and become a terrible headache. Hunched over her desk all day she had declined Dr. Clara's offer of breakfast and Henry and Liza's offer of picking her up a sandwich for lunch. Surviving only on tea or coffee with buckets of sugar, Sofia was determined to not only fix the mistake Professor Shipley had pointed out to her, but also build another block of data that would blow his mind. She desperately wanted to redeem herself. She was smarter than this one mistake and she knew she was capable of doing great work. The problem was, things just weren't flowing.

Sofia sighed for the thousandth time that day, having caught herself staring out the window at the rain that had dropped down over London and was not letting up. She kept getting distracted. Her computer screen glowed with a dozen different spreadsheets bursting with data. Several browser windows were also open, filled with computer code that she was reviewing, tweaking or testing. She had fixed the initial glitch that caused the problem in the report, that had been no big deal. But she was knee deep in creating the new information she hoped would impress Professor Shipley, and she was getting bogged down.

Looking back to her computer screen, the images blurred. She had to rub her eyes, which only made them blur more. She'd been staring at screens too long. No wonder her eyes kept wandering out the window. They were tired. She was tired.

Sofia leaned back and stretched the kinks out of her shoulders. The back of her wheeled desk chair squeaked in defiance. Pushing the chair away from her desk, she turned it on the hard wood floor so she was facing the large table in the center of the room. Liza was alone there, tapping away at her laptop.

Sofia glanced at the darkened doorways of Professor Shipley's and Dr. Clara's offices, then back to Liza. "Are we the only ones here?"

Liza didn't answer, just kept typing away. A thin black wire hung down from under her hair and dropped to the laptop where it was plugged in. Ear buds. Sofia waved at her and the motion caught Liza's attention.

She stopped typing, pulled the ear buds out of her ears and said, "Oh, hello! You've been busy, then?"

Sofia's eyes flicked to the clock on the wall. It read 4:26. She'd been holed up at her desk since 7:30 this morning. No wonder her eyes were tired.

"Yes, a little. Trying to push through a few things."

"Right," Liza smiled. Her dark bangs were flopped down over one eye, giving her a sort of floppy eared puppy dog look.

"Where's Henry?"

"He had to leave early today. Doctor appointment or something?"

A firm knock on the office door interrupted them. As they watched, the door pushed open and, much to Sofia's surprise, Ian stepped into the room.

He wore his signature worn jeans and black boots, along with an olive green long sleeve sweater over a white button up shirt. The sleeves were rolled and pushed up past his elbows so his tattoos were visible. Liza, being closest to the door, was the first person he saw.

"Hullo," he said politely. Then his eyes shifted to Sofia and warmed. "Hullo! I was hoping I had the right door."

Sofia couldn't help but notice Liza's shock and admiration upon seeing Ian in all of his impressive glory. The younger woman blushed and stammered. Ian, always cool and charming, included her in his warm smile after greeting Sofia. His eyes held a greenish gold hue today, probably because of the color of his sweater. Even in a sweater he had an edgy sexiness about him that screamed 'rock & roll'.

"What are you doing here?" Sofia asked accusingly. The surprise of seeing him brought all of her tension to the surface.

Ian's smile faltered, but only slightly, before he explained, "I've come by to see if you'd like to grab a bite."

Heat rose in Sofia's cheeks as Liza's wide eyes moved from Ian to Sofia. This was really too much. She was at work. He hadn't even called or texted to see if it was okay to drop by. Her embarrassment was fast boiling into anger. She couldn't take much more stress today. She was at her tipping point.

"I called...and texted...but you didn't answer. And I was in the neighborhood..." his voice trailed off as he could see that he was not being welcomed with open arms.

"I'm Liza," Liza said abruptly. She stood and offered her slim, pale hand to him.

He took it with a smile. "I'm Ian."

"You're a friend of Sofia's?" Liza said, politely trying to create conversation.

"Yes," Ian said, then he blushed endearingly. "Friend, yes." He cleared his throat and Sofia could tell that Liza knew the entire story of their relationship because of his stammering answer.

"Ian, I–" she started, but was stopped by the bumbling entrance of Dr. Clara into the room.

"Oh, pardon me," Dr. Clara said in her upbeat musical tone as she bumped into Ian in the doorway. She carried a purse and a laptop bag over her wide, awkward shoulder and her arms were full of books.

"No, pardon me," Ian said, stepping back. "Here, let me help you." He took the books from her and stepped out of her way.

"Thank you, so much. You can set them down anywhere,"

Dr. Clara said, waving her large hand happily toward the long table.

"This is Sofia's *friend*, Ian," Liza interjected.

"Oh, marvelous," Dr. Clara exclaimed. She extended her hand to Ian who graciously took it after placing the books on the table. "I'm Dr. Clara Weston."

"Ian...Ian Law," he gave her a small, informal bow as he shook her hand.

"Nice name," Dr. Clara said. She shot Sofia an approving look then shared an amused glance with Liza.

This needed to end.

"Ian, can I talk to you for a minute?" Sofia blurted out. All eyes turned to her in surprise at her tone. She didn't care. This was her job and she was not going to jeopardize it because Ian Law couldn't take no for an answer. "Outside?" She arched her brow at him.

Ian only hesitated for an instant before answering, "Of course." He turned to Dr. Clara and Liza, "Very nice meeting you both."

In the hallway Sofia spoke to him in a harsh whisper, "You can't come by my work!"

"Sorry, I'm sorry, I thought you might be done for the day." He looked her up and down, taking in her disheveled hair and pinched expression. "And might be hungry or tired..."

"I am hungry and I am tired," she said. She felt like crying, which made her furious. "And I have a headache and I have a job, Ian. A job that is very important to me."

"Of course," he said with sincerity. His kind do-good thing wrapped up in the appealing rock star package wasn't working for her right now. They were not dating and, more than that, she did not want to date some wannabe musician. It was time she made her feelings perfectly clear.

"I can't deal with this right now. I have a big project going on and this," she flapped her hands violently in his direction, "just stresses me out." Her voice had a tremor induced by fury and the tears that wanted to fall. "I don't want a boyfriend, I don't want to go out to dinner with you, and I don't want you to surprise me at work."

His face fell. Sofia couldn't look at him so she looked back toward the half open door to her office, wishing she could step away and close it so her conversation with Ian wouldn't be overheard. But that seemed like it would call too much attention to her, so she stayed where she was. When she turned back to Ian he had collected himself.

"Fair enough," he said. The greenish gold in his eyes glowed with admiration. "I know what it takes to make a dream come true." He glanced at her office door behind her back, then looked at her again. His eyes were smiling. "I also know that sometimes a person needs to let go a little, experience some of the beauty of the world." She started to say something, affronted that he would think her someone who didn't appreciate the beauty in the world. "Wait–" he held his finger up close to her mouth, shushing her. "If you change your mind, give me a call. I'd be happy to experience some of those things with you." Then, he turned around and walked away.

As she watched him retreat down the long hallway, the low mood she'd been in darkened even more. Her head was throbbing and she wished she could go home. She wished Ian would look back at her, but he didn't, and she did not call out to him to apologize or smooth things over. When he got to the end of the hallway, he hit the wide metal bar that opened the heavy doors with his palm and pushed it open. The sound echoed down the hall.

That's when she heard an unmistakable *harrumph* behind her.

Chapter Seventeen

Sofia whirled around to find Professor Shipley standing in the office doorway, watching her.

"Professor," she said, startled by his presence. She was mortified at the possibility that he had overheard her conversation with Ian.

"I have some questions on your newest attempt," he lifted the revised report she had printed.

With the air of a prisoner bravely facing the gallows, Sofia followed him back into the office. All of them ended up working late to appease Professor Shipley's expectations. The whole time, Sofia thought about how nice it might have been to go out to dinner with Ian.

By the time she made it to her flat that evening she was exhausted, starving, aching, and soaking wet. Her normal walk home had been plagued by the drizzling rain, which had added shivers and a stuffed up nose to her already throbbing headache.

"Great," she complained to nobody in the room as she opened the fridge to find it absolutely empty. She hadn't had time to go shopping when she got home from her weekend trip late last night. And today...she sighed...today had been long and awful. "Bath it is," she announced.

A half hour later she was feeling better. Sunk into a warm bath after popping a few ibuprofen for her headache, the pain was beginning to subside. She had fixed herself a cup of ginger tea that sat steaming on the edge of the tub. That and the hot bath had done the trick and she was finally warm again. Spanish guitar music floated through the small bathroom, emanating from her cell phone. She took a sip of her tea and noticed that her nail polish was chipping badly. She needed to get in for a manicure somewhere soon.

Suddenly her nose tickled furiously and she sat up in the tub. Unable to control herself, Sofia sneezed so powerfully that her bath water splashed over the edge. Her headache returned immediately.

"No, no, no, no..." she said under her breath. "I am *not* getting sick."

A knock sounded on the door of her flat.

After the initial surprise, she became indignant. Ian. Again. He was stalking her. Was she going to have to file a restraining order or something just to get some peace?

"Honestly," she muttered as she climbed out of the tub and threw on her bathrobe. From the time it took her to get out of the tub until she was reaching for the door handle, Sofia went from indignant to fuming. She unlocked the dead bolt and jerked the door open, not caring that she wasn't dressed. "What do you wa–" Sofia stopped short. Her mouth dropped open in surprise.

"Hi, cuz!" Luna's voice was high pitched and excited.

Sofia stared in shock at Luna with a carry on bag at her feet.

"I've come for a visit!" Luna announced. She waited a beat, then asked, "Are you going to let me in?"

Sofia was overcome at the surprise. Luna had kept the

whole thing under wraps despite usually sharing everything with her cousin. She had even enlisted Tawnyetta's help by getting exact directions to her flat.

"Can you believe she's pregnant?" Luna asked as she relayed her travel story to Sofia over her own mug of hot ginger tea.

"I know! It's so exciting!" Sofia was excited for Tawnyetta and Michael. She was also thrilled to have Luna here curled up on her couch in her little flat in London. It lifted her spirits in ways that little else could. "Are you going to spend any time going up to see them?"

"Scotland? Now?" Luna seemed surprised. Sofia nodded and sipped her tea. "No, no, this trip is just for you," Luna said as she reached out and patted Sofia's shoulder in a motherly way. "Everyone is anxious to know how you're settling in and I had some vacation time to spend, so I thought why not? Besides I'll see Tawnyetta when we go to her big fundraiser."

"By everyone do you mean my parents?" Sofia asked.

Luna smiled and nodded.

A wave of homesickness came over Sofia and she teared up. Her parents were fiercely protective and proud, but they were not the world traveling types. Thinking about how much she missed them, and they her, made her heartsick.

"Oh, don't be sad," Luna clucked at her like a hen with a chick. "They're fine. They're so proud of you, Sofia."

That sweet sentiment pushed her over the edge. Sofia broke down crying.

"What's going on with you?" Luna asked sweetly.

"I've had a horrible day. I got in trouble at work," Sofia tried to explain through her tears. Suddenly, she remembered another mistake she'd made. She grabbed Luna's arm with a gasp. "Oh, no!"

"What's wrong?"

"I forgot to give Tawnyetta's invitations to her fundraiser to the professors!" Sofia felt sick to her stomach at the failure.

Luna's brows pinched together. "That's not for a few months, right?"

Sofia's panic subsided slightly. "Yes, you're right. That's fine, isn't it? If I get them to the professors tomorrow?"

"Yes, I'm sure that's fine." Luna studied Sofia for a few moments before prodding her for more information. "What's really going?"

With the question, Luna triggered a release of all that Sofia had been struggling with since coming to London. Everything came out at once. Moving, adjusting to a new job, tension about her mistakes and feeling intimidated by Professor Shipley. Not to mention her feelings, be they what they were, about Ian. She dumped it all on poor little Luna, who cooed and cajoled and generally made her feel better. Finally, when Sofia was exhausted from emoting and a possible impending cold, and Luna was wiped out by jet lag, they went to bed. They shared the tiny double bed in Sofia's room like when they were little kids sleeping at their Abuela's house.

The next morning Sofia woke up with a full-blown head cold. Thank goodness Luna was there. Her sweet younger cousin took such good care of her, cooking for her, making sure she took medicine and drank herbal teas, running her hot baths and even finding her menthol rub for her chest that helped her breathe. Under Luna's care, Sofia was able to at least make it to work and get through the next few days. Although Luna would have preferred if she stayed home.

"I cand miss days, Luda," Sofia explained. When she spoke with her stuffed up nose, all of her 'n's' and 't's' sounded like the letter 'd'. "Dot with Professor Shipley breathing dowd my deck."

Together they got through the week and Sofia was on the

mend. She even managed to slip the invitations to the fundraiser at Castle Claymore for Tawnyetta into Professor Shipley and Dr. Clara's in boxes while they were out. At the end of the week, she and Luna received an invitation to another of Bea and Travis' increasingly infamous dinner parties.

Luna was thrilled. Sofia less so. In her short time in London, one of the staples of a Bea and Travis dinner party was Ian Law. And she wasn't sure if spending an evening with him was something she wanted, or even could handle at this point.

"We don't have to go," Luna offered. Though her mood was definitely dampened at the idea of refusing an evening with friends.

"I'll be fine. We should go," Sofia reassured her cousin. At least her nose wasn't as red and stuffed up as it had been during the week. Luna had tried to get her to talk about her feelings for Ian since Sofia brought him up on the first night. Luna already had her suspicions regarding their relationship since Thomas had shared the picture of Sofia and Ian on the London Eye a few weeks ago.

"So..." Luna said cautiously over a bowl of chicken tortilla soup she had whipped up while Sofia was at work. "You don't really like him after all?"

"No," Sofia said with assurance.

Luna gave her a little scowl. "I don't believe you."

Sofia's eyes flashed at being outed. She waved her soup spoon around in the air as she spoke. "I like him, okay? He's a nice person. He's fun and handsome and exciting. I'll give you all of that." Sofia pointed her spoon at Luna for emphasis. "But he's not for me. We are too different. I'm not a groupie type and he's, you know..."

"He's what?"

"He's an artist!" Sofia exclaimed, as if announcing he was

an alien life form and could not be considered as a possible mate.

"Okay, okay," Luna chuckled and changed the subject.

On Friday night as they entered Bea and Travis' home, Sofia was both anxious and excited to see Ian. Her stomach clenched at the memory of the first time she was there and he let her in the front door. The memory of him walking down the hallway at King's College the last time she saw him made her feel a little queasy. Too much had passed between them for her to be perfectly fine during dinner, but she was willing to do her best to be normal and polite for the sake of Bea and Travis and their hospitality. Plus she wanted Luna to have a nice evening out.

"How have you been?" Bea exclaimed as she hugged Luna and ushered them both into her home.

"I'm well, thank you," Luna answered. "How are you?"

"Oh, busy, busy, busy, as always," Bea's eyes shone. She loved having people over, this was obvious. "Well, come in, take your coats off. Travis is pouring the wine!"

As they entered the dining area and greeted Travis, Sofia steeled herself to run smack into Ian. To her surprise, they found Travis alone in the dining room pouring wine into four wine glasses. Four wine glasses placed neatly on a table set for four. Only four.

Sofia's resolve to be strong and calm while dining with Ian morphed into a need to act normal in the face of acute disappointment. As much as she had not wanted to deal with Ian and all of his tattooed good looks and sex appeal tonight, she felt a stab of bitter sadness when she realized he was not going to be there at all.

"Do tell me everything that's happening with everyone," Bea said to Luna.

Luna accepted a glass of red wine from Travis and thought

for a moment before responding, "Oh! Thomas is dating someone new."

Bea's eyes flew open with delight. "Really? Who is the lucky girl?"

"Her name is Marin. She's very nice," Luna said before taking a sip of her wine. She swallowed and said, "Bridget hates her."

They all laughed. Bridget didn't always like it when anyone else got too much attention.

"And is Bridget seeing anyone?" Bea inquired.

"Actually, she's dabbled in online dating a bit."

"Really?" Bea lifted her eyebrows in surprise. "Does she like it?"

Luna shrugged, "A little. She gets a lot of attention, but not always the best kind."

"Just us four for dinner?" Sofia asked. All eyes turned to her and she realized that it was an awkward question.

Bea and Travis shared a nearly imperceptible look, but not so imperceptible that Sofia and Luna didn't see it. Sofia blushed.

"Yes, dear," Bea said sweetly. "It's just us four tonight. Even numbers are good luck!"

Sofia nodded and tried to act like she hadn't just upped the awkward dial in the room. Luna watched her, a queer look in her eyes.

"Speaking of numbers–" Travis started, turning to Sofia.

"I suppose you're used to having Ian here with us," Bea interrupted.

Sofia blushed harder and said, "Yes, I guess that's it."

"Of course," Bea's bright demeanor dimmed with sympathy. "He would have made it I'm sure, if he'd been able." She leaned toward Luna and confided, "Ian's a good friend of ours. Very entertaining. But he's becoming quite the big rock star these days. Can't always make it to little get togethers like this anymore. He's being interviewed on the radio next week!"

Travis watched to make sure Bea was finished talking before addressing Sofia a second time, "Speaking of numbers–"

"We'll just have to do without him tonight I guess. Have our own sing-alongs!" Bea exclaimed delightedly. Travis sighed and waited as Bea started toward the kitchen. "More stuffed pork, stewed apples, and goat cheese mashed potatoes for the rest of us," she declared as she disappeared into the kitchen.

"Can I help you with anything?" Luna asked, following her.

Travis watched the two women until they were both safely in the kitchen. Then he gave Sofia an apologetic smile. He lifted the wine bottle and offered Sofia a top off. She declined with a shake of her head. He topped off his own while glancing at her empathetically.

"I don't suppose you really want to know about Ian?" he asked.

She shook her head again, "No, not really."

"Very well," Travis set the bottle of wine back on the table. "Speaking of numbers..." he began and led a grateful Sofia into a thoroughly Information Technology based conversation about her work, avoiding all references to the rock star missing from the dinner party.

Chapter Eighteen

Luna's trip was short, but needed. When she flew back to the states the following week, Sofia watched her go with a healing heart. Her cousin had shown up at a low point and not only nursed her back to physical health, but helped Sofia rebound from homesickness and lovesickness.

"I'll be back in less than two months for the fundraiser and everyone will be together again at the castle," Luna told her when they were saying their goodbyes.

"I know, that will be fun," Sofia said. And she meant it. She had that visit to look forward to and she felt invigorated to face the challenges of her job for the next few months on her own.

The weather was shifting into fall in London. This meant a drop in temperature and more rain than she was used to coming from the more arid climate of Colorado. Sofia spruced up her wardrobe a bit with a new wide collared, button up, Burgundy wool jacket. She thought the splash of fall color would help improve her mood. She also made more than a few visits to The Red Lion book shop and bought several new and gently used titles to keep her mind occupied during the fall nights at home.

Work was improving. Or, more specifically, work with Professor Shipley was improving. She didn't make any more inexcusable mistakes and he was pleased with her work in general. He was also more receptive than she expected him to be upon receiving the invitation to Tawnyetta's fundraiser ball.

"Claymore Castle?" he asked from the doorway of his office after he found the invitation in his inbox.

Sofia smiled nervously. "Yes, my friends asked me to invite you and Dr. Clara."

He tilted his chin down so that he was peering at her over the top of his glasses. "You're friends with Lord and Lady MacBrody?"

She nodded. Liza and Henry had stopped their work and were observing the exchange with wide eyes. Dr. Clara appeared in the doorway to her office holding her invitation.

"I think it's marvelous. What a chance to see the Scottish countryside and go to a gala," she smiled widely, her tiny eyes squinting with the pleasure of it all. "We should all go together!" She looked to Sofia for a response and Sofia could only nod in agreement. Dr. Clara then realized a potential problem. Turning to Henry and Liza, she asked, "Would you both be interested in going to a fundraiser ball?" Henry and Liza looked at each other then back to Dr. Clara.

"In Scotland?" Liza asked.

"Yes, yes, in Scotland," Dr. Clara's deep voice was benevolent.

Liza looked shyly at Sofia and nodded. "That would be very nice indeed."

"How about you, Henry?" Dr. Clara encouraged the young man to speak up.

Taking his cue from Liza, Henry nodded and said, "Yes, sure, why not?"

Dr. Clara pointed at Sofia with her invitation and asked, "If Frederick and I bring them as our plus ones, will that do for Lord and Lady MacBrody?"

Sofia, though a little surprised at how the fundraiser ball had suddenly become an office retreat, didn't see why Tawnyetta or Michael would mind. "I don't think that would be a problem."

Dr. Clara beamed. "Excellent. It's settled then. We'll take the train. I'll check the dates."

"What if I want to bring someone else as my guest?" Professor Shipley asked, insulted at Dr. Clara's presumption.

"Oh, Frederick, you don't have a plus one," she said lightly as she waved her invitation at him, dismissing his argument.

"I beg your pardon–" Professor Shipley began to argue.

"Stop being a curmudgeon," Dr. Clara called out to him as she retreated back into her office.

Professor Shipley called after her, "Clara!"

"You don't have a plus one, Frederick. Stop pretending that you do!" Dr. Clara's voice emerged from somewhere out of sight.

Sofia, Henry, and Liza sat in stunned silence as Professor Shipley harrumphed, stepped back into his office and slammed the door shut.

Henry was the first to speak. "What the hell just happened?"

Liza looked from Henry to Sofia and then at Professor Shipley's closed door. "I guess it's all settled, then," she repeated Dr. Clara's words.

They all cracked up laughing.

Everything wasn't quite settled, however, because Sofia needed to find a dress for the ball. And she had very little money to spend. As it turned out, Liza was in the same predicament. Dr. Clara had 'an old black velvet number that should do nicely', so she was covered. Sofia turned to the only person she thought might be able to help her and Liza with their predicament. Bea.

"Oh, yes," Bea told her excitedly when she called. "I know some great places we can go to get second hand dresses that you would never guess had been previously worn. I could use a new gown myself, come to think of it. I think my old evening wear has outgrown me...or vice versa!"

That's how Travis, Bea, Sofia, Liza and Henry ended up on a Saturday afternoon shopping spree in Fitzrovia. Travis had come along to carry their packages and Henry had been invited as a companion for Travis while the ladies shopped. Although Sofia and Bea believed he agreed to accompany the shopping party because he had a crush on Liza. Which was adorable.

"Liza, do you like this blue?" Bea held up a bright blue gown with piles of ruffles falling like foam to the floor. Liza paled at the sight of it.

"I think that might be a bit bright for Liza," Sofia suggested. "And with all those ruffles it might swallow her up."

Bea turned the gown back to look it over again. "True, true."

As they searched through racks of gently used discounted designer dresses, Travis and Henry sat in the waiting area looking at their phones.

"What color do you want, Sofia?" Liza asked in her thin, high voice.

"Black," Sofia answered without a thought. "I love black and then I can wear it again and again."

"Isn't black a little dreary?" Bea piped up. "I mean, you have such beautiful skin tone, you could wear brighter colors if you wanted."

Sofia spied a beautiful vintage grey lace tiered dress that looked about Liza's size and pulled it off the rack. Just as she was lifting it to show the younger woman, an uncanny sound reached her ears. It was the sound of Ian...singing.

Sofia spun around to see where the music might be coming from, but there was no stage in the large, well-lit thrift store. There wasn't even any music pumping through the speakers for the discount shoppers to enjoy. No, the music was coming from someplace else nearby. That's when she spied Henry holding his phone up for Travis to see and, apparently, hear what it was playing. Sofia went to them, unable to contain her curiosity. Her heart beat harder than she would care to admit the closer she got to them.

Sure enough, as she got nearer she could hear the chorus.

Shine on me, shine on me, bring me your light.
Take my heart, take my breath, take my life.

Travis did a double take when he saw her approaching, but Henry was controlling the phone.

"Sofia, have a listen. Have you heard this band? The Tellers?" Henry asked.

Sofia nodded, "Yes, I have."

"So has Travis! What are the odds of that? They were playing at the club a few weeks ago. Bloody awesome, they were," Henry pushed his finger on a button on his phone and the song Sofia was almost positive Ian had written for her stopped playing. "That song's a bit slow. Here's a good one." Another song Sofia recognized started up. Travis was watching her with concern.

"We don't have to listen–" Travis started to say.

"No, it's fine," Sofia insisted. "I like them." She smiled at Henry who did not notice her reaction to hearing Ian. Travis noticed, but when he looked like he was about to say something to Henry to change the music, Sofia shook her head at him. "It's fine," she smiled insistently.

But it wasn't fine. Not really. She'd gone days without allowing any thoughts of Ian to enter her head. Hearing him sing brought everything back. Memories of him on stage electrifying her and an entire crowd of people, singing alone with his guitar with such emotion she felt like her soul was being pulled out of her body, in Bea's living room sitting so close to her she could feel the heat emanating from his body while he sang her song. All of this and more flooded through her mind and swept through her core. She missed him. She missed him so much.

"What have you got there?" Bea's voice cut through Sofia's misery.

Bea had joined them and was looking at the dress Sofia held in her hands. The grey tiered dress she thought might be perfect for Liza. She held it out and managed, "For Liza."

"That's perfect!" Bea exclaimed then held up her own discovery for Sofia, a white tulle sleeveless dress with a pattern of black birds in flight sewn across the top layer. The birds flew thinner at the hem and neckline and closer together at the waist, making it two toned–very sleek and elegant. "And this would be perfect on you!"

The next few weeks were astonishingly busy. It took a lot to organize a train trip for seven people across the United Kingdom and have them arrive prepared to spend a full weekend and attend a black tie event. The ladies even had to have their gowns shipped ahead of time because they wouldn't have room to pack them onto the train. When Sofia thought they were done planning everything, Luna called and told her she wanted to come to London first and travel with her to Claymore Castle. So their party of seven became a party of eight.

"We must take the Caledonian Sleeper train," Dr. Clara insisted during a working lunch when they were finalizing plans for the trip. "It's nearly 13 hours to Inverness. I hear their new cars are outstanding."

Sofia was excited about that idea. Traveling across the countryside in a train sounded lovely. Romantic. Ian crossed her mind and she squelched the thought, which made her sad. She sighed and muttered a rebuke under her breath, "Stop it."

"What's that?" Dr. Clara's beady eyes blinked at her.

"Nothing, the sleeper train sounds nice," Sofia answered.

There was the uncomfortable issue of dual occupancy. Bea and Travis would share a berth, naturally. Now that Luna was joining them, Sofia would share a berth with her cousin. That left Dr. Clara, Professor Shipley, Henry, and Liza. There was no automatic pairing that made sense except to split them up by gender. That meant Liza would bunk with Dr. Clara and Henry would bunk with Professor Shipley.

"Bloody hell," Henry complained. They had all grown much more comfortable with each other over the past weeks of working and planning together. Plus, Professor Shipley wasn't present at this lunch, so Henry felt free to express his feelings. "I've got to share with Shipley?" He grimaced at the idea.

"Now, now, we can't very well push you and Liza in a berth for a work trip. That wouldn't be exactly proper, would it?" Dr. Clara explained in her upbeat way.

Liza blushed and Henry fidgeted. Sofia was pretty sure they would rather be with each other than with Professor Shipley or Dr. Clara. But this way was more professional.

"How is this a work trip again?" Liza asked.

Dr. Clara leaned back in her chair and used her best lecture voice, "Well, we have been asked to this event as representatives of King's College. And you," here she indicated Henry, Liza, and Sofia with a sweep of her arm, "are going along as representatives as well...except you," she nodded at Sofia with a smile. "You're friends with the Lord and Lady already."

Sofia was glad for the distraction this trip provided. But the truth was, it couldn't distract her completely because she knew that Ian would be performing at the ball. She hoped that having her bosses and coworkers there, Bea and Travis, as well as Luna, Angie, Thomas and Bridget, would give her enough people to interact with that she could successfully avoid Ian. Plus, Tawnyetta's pregnancy was going to be a major focus. Bridget wanted to throw her a baby shower since all of her American friends would already be present. With all of that to keep her occupied, Sofia was almost one hundred percent certain she would be fine.

Almost.

As they boarded the train, used their keycards to enter their berths, and settled in for the overnight trip to Inverness, Sofia's stomach churned. She couldn't blame it on motion sickness, because the train wasn't moving yet. The problem was that every time she thought about the last time she saw Ian perform at Claymore Castle, she couldn't help but feel an intense mixture of excitement and dread. Excitement because she would get to be near him and feel the way he made her feel. Dread because she knew it was going to tear her heart into pieces.

Chapter Nineteen

S mashed into the small car shuttling them to the castle, Sofia tried to decipher what their driver, Allen, was saying. She remembered his thick Scottish accent from her previous trip to Claymore Castle, but had forgotten how impossible it was to understand him.

Sofia sat in the front passenger seat with Liza perched in the middle between her and Allen. Luna, Dr. Clara, and Professor Shipley were squashed into the back seat in that order. Bea and Travis were hiring a rental car and bringing Henry with them. Occasionally Dr. Clara would lean her large frame into the front seat in order to ask Allen or Sofia questions. This disruption wreaked havoc on the comfort of the others in the back seat, especially Professor Shipley, but Dr. Clara didn't seem to notice.

"Tirna ban sauna bok tu ere," Allen said. Nobody knew what he was saying, which made Sofia smile.

"So charming, quite charming, don't you think?" Doctor Clara exclaimed before dropping back and wriggling into her place between Luna and Professor Shipley. Professor Shipley grumbled something that Sofia couldn't hear. Dr. Clara chuckled. Sofia was beginning to suspect that Dr. Clara enjoyed getting a rise out of Professor Shipley whenever possible. It must be how she had managed to work with him day in, day out, for so many years.

"Oh my," Liza said under her breath as Claymore Castle came into view.

It had been a long time since Sofia was here with Tawnyetta and all of their friends. That vacation had been amazing. It all started when Bridget became a runaway bride and brought Tawnyetta on her honeymoon to Claymore Castle instead of her cheating ex-fiancé. A glorious two-week holiday turned into an epic love story where Lord Michael MacBrody and Tawnyetta fell in love. The whole trip had been a truly life changing event for Tawnyetta, and for all of them really. Without Claymore Castle Sofia wouldn't know Bea and Travis, she wouldn't she be coming to this grand event with her boss and coworkers...and she would never have met Ian.

The conversations of the other passengers melted into the background as they got closer. She wondered if Ian was already there, if she would see him right away or could she avoid him until she saw him perform at the ball. And which scenario did she want? As the great stone walls and towers of Claymore Castle grew larger, so the butterflies in Sofia's stomach grew more active.

"Beautiful," Luna said. She had leaned forward this time and was peering at the castle through the windshield. She looked at Sofia, "It's still hard to imagine that this is Tawnyetta's home now, isn't it?"

"Yes," Sofia agreed. "I haven't been up here to see them since the wedding."

"They got married here?" Liza was star struck.

"Ech to fee nar 'te wee bairn," said Allen with a chuckle. Luna and Sofia shared an amused look.

When they arrived, Tawnyetta met them at the door. It

was easy to see she had fallen into the role of Lady of the house with grace and style. Maybe it was the title, maybe it was the fact that she was a married woman, or maybe it was because she was happily pregnant with her first child, but Tawnyetta simply glowed. Sofia felt calmer just seeing her on the steps. Her friend was fully in her element and Sofia was excited once again for all of the festivities they were going to enjoy.

As the car stopped and they got out, Tawnyetta greeted them, "I'm so glad you're here. All of you." She hugged Sofia and Luna and shook hands warmly with the others. Sofia could see that her colleagues were smitten with Lady MacBrody. And when Lord MacBrody, or Laird MacBrody as he was known here, arrived on the scene they all got a little star struck, even Professor Shipley.

"Welcome, please come in," Michael said as he gallantly ushered them into his family's castle.

They barely got through the front door and greeted Stewart, the butler, when a high-pitched squeal emanated from the end of the Great Hall.

"Fiiiifiii! Luuuluu!"

Sofia and Luna turned to see Bridget rushing to greet them, her blonde curls bouncing, her blue eyes bright with joy. She was followed closely by the flowing, graceful Angie, her red hair wild and unkempt as it tumbled every which way down her back.

Sofia was overjoyed to be with all of her best friends again. Though, there was one missing.

"Where's Thomas?" she asked.

Bridget's pretty lips pouted as she threw a dirty look toward the spiral staircase at the end of the Great Hall that led to the honeymoon suite in the castle keep. "He's up there...with his new girlfriend. In our old room!" Bridget gave Tawnyetta an incensed look.

"He requested that room, Bridge," Tawnyetta said sooth-ingly. "He really likes Marin."

Bridget scowled and leaned toward Sofia as if sharing a big secret. "I don't like Marin."

Sofia laughed, "I gather that."

Bridget, Angie, and Tawnyetta helped Sofia and Luna settle into the room they were sharing. It was a second story bedroom with the grey stone outside walls boasting two massive windows that gave the best view of the formal gardens below. Two Queen size four-poster beds didn't even make the room seem cramped. They had pale blue silk bed curtains that could be closed for privacy and thick royal blue comforters with white lace pillow cases and more cozy blankets folded at the foot of the bed in the same pale blue as the curtains. The coffered ceilings were made of dark stained wood that matched the furnishings and the floors were polished stone covered with a thick blue and white rug. They had their own fireplace and en suite, complete with plush Claymore Castle bathrobes and slippers.

"Everything a girl could need," Luna said happily as she put her toiletries away.

"And your gowns came!" Bridget opened a large wardrobe to reveal two large hanging travel bags. "I peeked," Bridget admitted. "They're gorgeous! I'm wearing a vintage pink off the shoulder. It's very Pride and Prejudice." She told this specifically to Luna who nodded her approval. "We're all going to be just beautiful tonight," Bridget beamed.

"How are you, Sofia?" Angie plopped down on one of the beds and patted the space next to her for Sofia to sit down. "Do you like London?"

Sofia sat down, appreciating the comfortable mattress. "I do, it has a lot going on all the time, which is nice. Work is going well. A little bumpy to start off, but its been getting better."

"All of your coworkers came with you, didn't they?" Angie asked. Sofia nodded. "How fun!" Angie offered, though Sofia wasn't sure it was as fun as her friend made it sound.

Bridget had a thought. "Are there any eligible bachelors among them?"

Sofia screwed up her mouth thoughtfully. "Well, there's Henry, but he's still in school. And I think he likes Liza."

"He definitely likes Liza," Luna giggled.

Bridget waved her hand, dismissing the subject. "Well, that doesn't matter anyway because we have a wonderful party tonight..." she moved to Tawnyetta's side and gave her a sideways hug. "And we have Tawny's baby shower tomorrow!"

All of them turned to Tawnyetta, which made her redden. "All right, all right, that's tomorrow. I have a million things to do today before all of the guests arrive this evening." She unconsciously rested her hand on her slightly rounded belly as she spoke.

"What can we do to help?" Luna asked.

Tawnyetta did have a lot to do, but with the assistance of her staff and handing off more personal tasks to her friends, the preparations for the fundraiser ball continued smoothly. She specifically asked Sofia to check in on Professor Shipley and Dr. Clara to ensure they had everything they needed. Sofia agreed, happy to have something to do to keep her mind off of Ian. She headed toward the rooms that her university friends had been assigned.

"I'm with Shipley again," Henry said as soon as she saw him in the hall. After sharing a berth on the train with his boss, Sofia was sure Henry had had enough of Professor Shipley.

"I'm sorry, Henry," Sofia offered. She put her hand on his shoulder in condolence.

"It wouldn't be so bad if he didn't snore so bloody loud," Henry grumbled.

Sofia had to suppress a laugh. She tried to think of something encouraging to say. It seemed that both Henry and Liza looked to her as a kind of supervisor or big sister who could guide them through sticky situations with the professors.

"You have the ball tonight," she said. "You can stay out practically all night having a good time and you won't have to listen to his snoring." Henry shrugged, his head drooped. Maybe distracting him with romance would help. "Liza will be at the ball, too. I'm sure she will be happy to stay out with you, dancing and having a good time."

Henry snapped his eyes to hers, dread filling his features. "Dancing?" he asked. Sofia nodded. He swallowed, sending his Adam's apple up and down his long, pale neck and asked, "Ballroom dancing?"

Sofia could see this was a problem for him. "Well...yes...at least during the first part of the evening." Her thoughts flew to Ian who would be performing the second show of the evening. "But then it will be more like club dancing." Henry's face grew paler, if that was possible. "You dance, don't you?" Sofia asked, though she was sure she already knew the answer by the look on his face.

"Bloody hell," he said, though it came out as a kind of choked whisper.

"Don't you go to clubs?"

Henry nodded as he ran his thin fingers through his dark, floppy hair. "Yes, but I don't bloody dance," he admitted. "I don't know how!" Again he whispered. A pathetic, plaintive sound.

"I'm sorry, Henry," Sofia said with pity. She wished she could think of some way to help him.

Henry made a fist and pounded it gently onto his forehead. "I should have listened to my Mum. She said I should take lessons."

Sofia nodded sympathetically. "My Dad taught me. He

insisted. He used to let me stand on his feet when I was little, but eventually I got the idea."

"You know how to waltz?"

"Yes, and fox trot, and salsa." She didn't mention belly dancing, though Angie had drug her to enough classes as a drop in that she could confidently say she knew at least the basics.

Suddenly, Henry grabbed her arm and gave her a beseeching look. "Can you teach me?"

"What?"

"Teach me...please! I'll be forever grateful."

"But the ball is less than eight hours away!"

"I'm a fast learner."

Sofia hesitated. "I don't know..." she said, but she did know. Looking into Henry's pleading eyes, she knew she would do what she could to help him out. And with just hours to work with, she also knew they needed to get started right away.

Chapter Twenty

They gathered in the weapons room. Sofia originally thought the ballroom was a more obvious choice, but Henry didn't want everyone in the castle to witness his attempts at dancing. So they settled on the less used, low traffic, weapons room. It had a wide marble floor in the center used for sword practice that would do nicely for dancing.

What had started as a one-on-one tutorial by Sofia to instruct Henry quickly turned into a larger group hoping to improve their skills before the ball that evening. Dr. Clara and Professor Shipley joined to get in some practice.

Travis showed up unexpectedly as well. Clearing his throat before asking, "I wonder if you might show me a step or two? I thought it might be a nice surprise for Bea if I took her on a few turns around the dance floor."

"Of course!" Sofia was delighted at the idea. "That leaves us one lady short. I'll see if Bridget can join us."

Bridget, an accomplished dancer starting at age four when she started in ballet and tap, agreed whole-heartedly. So did Luna, who had learned from her uncle alongside Sofia when they were little. This left Sofia without a partner, which turned out to be good because she needed all of her concentration to watch the group of dancers as they practiced.

"That's it, one-two-three, one-two-three," she moved alongside Bridget and Henry as they stepped to the music. "Very nice, Henry," she complimented him and his cheeks turned even redder than they had when the beautiful Bridget had been chosen as his dance partner. Embarrassed as he was, he was definitely catching on quickly.

That was not the case with Travis. When his wife told everyone that he could not dance she was not exaggerating. Tall and awkward, stiff in his mannerisms and worrying so much about keeping count that he forgot to take steps, Travis was not making strides. With just hours until the ball, Sofia worried he wouldn't be able to dance with Bea after all.

Luna, bless her sweet heart, was patient with him. "Just take a deep breath," she told him quietly while she paused after he stepped on her toe for the umpteenth time that afternoon.

"I'm so sorry. I'm probably a lost cause," he let his arms drop to his sides.

"Don't give up!" Dr. Clara called out to him as she and Professor Shipley waltzed past. She was at least six inches taller than the other women in the room, but she moved her larger frame as gracefully as anyone. "It's glorious once you get the hang of it!" She smiled at Professor Shipley who seemed to be focusing on not leading her into the other couples. "Isn't it glorious, Frederick?"

Professor Shipley was a bit out of breath, but determined to keep in time with the music. "Hush, woman, I'm concentrating."

"You can't give up, Travis," Luna encouraged her defeated partner. "Bea will be over the moon if you just get the basics. We can do that, I'm sure of it."

"I think you're looking a lot better than when you first started today," Sofia added.

"Really?" Travis looked up, daring to be hopeful.

"Yes, much better. You are good at this, which doesn't surprise me." Sofia wanted to tell Travis something that would help. Maybe relating it back to the one thing she knew he felt more comfortable with, numbers, would give him the confidence he needed. "Besides, dancing is just numbers taken off the page, off the computer screen, and using them in the 3D world...with a little style thrown in."

Travis tilted his head and grinned, "I suppose that's true."

"I'll start a new song," Sofia went to her phone that was hooked up to a speaker Henry had brought to amplify the music. She chose the rousing Voices of Spring by Strauss. Soon all three dance pairs were swirling around the weapons room. If not overly graceful, at least they were moving without stumbling or stepping out of time. Sofia swayed to the music as she watched them. She had always loved to dance. In the past few years she hadn't taken much time to get out and do much of anything, let alone ballroom dance.

Closing her eyes for a moment, Sofia lifted her eyebrows as the sound of the strings lifted and fell, lifted and fell. The song pulled her along and made her feel light as a feather. Suddenly, she felt the weight of someone's gaze on her skin. She opened her eyes to see Ian leaning casually on one of the sword display cases on the other side of their makeshift dance floor. Her heart skipped a beat at the sight of him and a shiver rushed down her spine.

He had grown a beard since she'd last seen him. Had it been that long? His beard was the same deep red as his hair, maybe a little darker, and cut short so the square lines of his jaw were still very much visible. He wore a long sleeve black Henley shirt with the sleeves pushed up past his elbows. The black made the gold in his eyes stand out even more than normal and they glittered as he looked at her, a smile playing at the corners of his mouth.

Her hand fluttered to her chest, as if she was feeling for her heartbeat. The others continued dancing because the music was still playing, in fact it seemed to be playing even louder. Sofia found that she couldn't quite catch her breath as she watched Ian break into a grin and push himself off of the display case, making his way around the dancers to where she stood rooted to the floor.

When he reached her he made a slight bow. "It's good to see you," he said.

The sound of his voice sent another shiver through her body. Being this close to him again was intoxicating. She still couldn't breathe.

The song ended and just as she thought perhaps the whole dance lesson would dissipate and she could escape Ian's gaze, a new song started. Another waltz by Strauss. The Blue Danube. The introduction of the song began delightfully through Henry's small, but powerful, speakers. Music wrapped around Sofia and she lost track of what her dancing pupils were doing. Her eyes were glued to Ian.

He watched her steadily, not smiling, not frowning, soaking her up with his eyes. Sofia couldn't look away. She couldn't smile or speak. He was looking into her, searching for something. Or waiting for it. He let his gaze leave hers for a few moments as it traced her cheeks and mouth, brushing them with his attention so singularly that she thought she could feel the tickle of his touch on her skin. When he lifted his eyes to hers, they shone with desire, dark and molten.

Ian lifted his hand formally in front of her. A hand wrapped in tattoos and silver rings. Elegant, strong, masculine. This was the hand of a rebel, a musician, an artist. It was a silent request to dance. Beckoning her to join him, to trust him on the dance floor.

Without thinking of the consequences, Sofia lifted her hand. Her fingers trembled as they reached toward his. One corner of Ian's mouth twitched and his face softened into a crooked smile. Before she could change her mind, he took hold of her hand. The warmth of his skin sent a charge through her body. A shock of pure excitement that made her insides buzz.

The tempo of the song quickened, setting them up for the dance. Ian pulled her to him and lifted her hand into the air in perfect waltz position. She raised her other hand to his shoulder as he slowly, ever so slowly, slipped his around her body. His palm, placed underneath her shoulder blade on her back, held her firmly. His touch was strong, but gentle. His shoulder muscles were round and firm under her fingers. She had to stop herself from slipping her hand along his shoulder to his neck to touch the tattoo that twisted there, red roses wrapped in angry chains. Sofia's breath had returned, but it came quick and shallow.

The intro ended with three deep notes. Then came the unmistakable pause of The Blue Danube, the moment that simply hangs in the air just before the powerful music swells. Sofia stood in perfect form, heart pounding. Ian pressed his palm against her back, bringing her two inches closer to his chest so that they almost touched, but not quite. Sofia's eyes opened wider and she let out a small gasp. Their bodies were so close she could feel the warmth of his chest through her shirt. Ian grinned at her and, just as the waltz began, he gave her a conspiratorial wink. They began to dance.

He led her smoothly, skimming the floor and gracefully twirling with the other less competent couples. She was lost in the movement, in the feel of him using the slightest press of his palm or touch of his hand to make her go exactly where he wanted her to go. Just like when she was a little girl standing on her father's feet, it seemed as if she was lifted off of the ground. The music was enchanted, as if magic had infiltrated the notes. When she was little, she had imagined that magic could change her from a nervous schoolgirl into a beautiful lady floating across the dance floor.

But she was no longer a little girl. Not anymore.

And Ian was not her father.

Their feet flew under them as the song continued its famous strains. Ian held her eyes with his, each step, each twirl, binding them together. Mesmerized.

A sudden call broke the spell.

"Oi!" It was Henry, pointing at them from where he stood on the side of the marble floor. "You're Ian Law, aren't you?"

Sofia slowed to a stop, no longer taking cues from Ian. He came to a stop alongside her. They were both slightly out of breath.

Bridget stood next to Henry and, though she wasn't pointing, she was staring with great interest at the two of them. Sofia felt heat rise in her cheeks as she realized all of the dance class participants had stopped their own practicing and had been watching her and Ian.

"Bravo, Dr. Venegas!" Dr. Clara clapped her meaty hands together at Sofia and Ian. Ian grinned and did a partial bow before gesturing to Sofia as if she was the star.

"You are, you're Ian Law, aren't you?" Henry continued his single-minded questioning.

"At your service," Ian turned to Henry.

"From the Tellers?" Henry was impressed.

Ian's eyes crinkled in a good-natured wince. "The Robot Tellers," he corrected him.

Sofia glanced at Travis and Luna. Neither said anything but both had the same amused, knowing expressions on their faces. Sofia's brow pinched into a tiny scowl. She was never going to hear the end of this.

"Hello, do you remember me? I'm Bridget," Bridget

extended her hand to Ian who took it, averted his eyes politely to the floor at her feet and gave her a partial bow. As he did, Bridget took in the tattoos on his hand and arm that disappeared underneath his black shirt. She looked quickly at Sofia and raised her eyebrows, intrigued.

"How could I forget," Ian said as he straightened.

Bridget gave him a charming smile. She gave Sofia a meaningful look and continued, "I am dying to know how you and Fifi met." She looked back and forth between Sofia and Ian, "You do know each other, don't you?"

Ian looked at Sofia quizzically and asked, "Fifi?"

"Lesson is over!" Sofia called out to the group. A groan lifted from them, but she was not going to be deterred. "We only have three hours until dinner and less than five until the ball. No more dance lessons. You all passed with flying colors. Now I need some time to get ready."

And with that, Sofia took her things and hurried out the door with Luna and Bridget close on her heels. As the door to the weapons room closed slowly behind them, she glanced back and saw that Ian and Travis were watching them leave. Travis with a sort of placid amusement. Ian with a cocky smile.

Chapter Twenty-One

Preparing for a formal party under normal circumstances could be quite an event. Preparing for a ball in a Scottish castle with only three hours to get ready and Bridget at the helm was controlled chaos. She convinced Sofia, Luna, and Angie that they should get ready together in one room like when they were teenagers. So they brought all of their toiletries, makeup, undergarments, hair supplies, shoes, and gowns into Bridget and Angie's room and set about making themselves beautiful. The whole space was a glory of fabric, sweet smells, giggling, and jostling for room at the mirror.

"Tawnyetta is getting ready with Michael," Bridget explained from the bathroom. "She needs some peace and quiet before the big night anyway. She doesn't need to get over tired in her condition."

Sofia shared a look with Luna, because they knew what the other was thinking...*Lucky Tawnyetta.*

"What do you think?" Angie held a sparkling aquamarine blue gown up for them to see. Form fitted down to mid-thigh, the bodice and spaghetti straps were encrusted with shimmering beads ranging from tiny to pea sized. Starting mid-thigh there were what looked like pale green seashells attached to the fabric and holding long white wisps of tulle that swept down to the floor like a waterfall and made up the skirt.

"Angie, that's gorgeous!" Luna exclaimed.

Angie beamed. "We found it at a vintage place. Bridget got hers there, too."

"Ta-da!" Bridget stepped out of the bathroom on cue donning a pale pink, off the shoulder, empress waist gown that wrapped around her bosom, pushing it up where nobody could miss it even if they tried. There were tiny puffs of material across the bust of the fabric that then draped across her arms and looked like dozens of roses spilling over her skin. The higher waist of the dress started just under her bosom, allowing the skirt to drop to the floor in long, elegant lines of the same pale pink.

"Very nice," Sofia said. "I got mine at a second hand store in London, but I don't know if it's vintage or not."

"Just you saying 'second hand store in London' makes it sound so worldly!" Bridget said with delight.

"Well, mine is brand new, but I think it still looks a little old fashioned," Luna went to the wardrobe and pulled out her gown. It was a deep orange, but still light and airy with mounds of orange and white tulle for a skirt. The bodice was simple, strapless, but had the same orange and white tulle attached to one side that would drape over her left shoulder and fall down her back like a stole.

"That's such a beautiful color," Bridget said. She turned to Sofia's dress with its white tulle skirt and black overlay of bird silhouettes. "This is stunning, Fifi. I think it might be an Oscar de la Renta." As Bridget hunted along the inside seams for a tag that would verify her guess, Sofia took her turn in the bathroom mirror.

Quiet. For a few moments anyway. Sofia took a deep breath and looked at her reflection.

Blowing the air out through her mouth, she was surprised at the calmness of her expression. There were no extra creases on her brow, no lines at the corners of her eyes, nothing that would belie the truth of what was happening inside her at this very minute. She stared into her eyes. Green like emeralds, her father had always said. She leaned closer to the mirror to look deeper into them, to see if any of the powerful emotions that were still pulsing through her body since Ian had released her on the dance floor could be seen by the naked eye. Nothing.

Wait. There was something. Deep in the ocean of her eyes she saw it. A sparkle. A glimmer of what she could only call hope. Hope that something magical was happening between her and Ian. Hope that he would dance with her again at the ball. Hope that maybe, just maybe, there was a happy ending possible for them after all.

Bridget popped her blonde head in the bathroom door. "It is Oscar de la Renta!"

Sofia smiled. Lifted by Bridget's enthusiasm, she did her hair and makeup. She decided to keep her hair loose, teasing and adding product to give it more volume than normal as it cascaded over her bare shoulders and back. She wore a black velvet choker with a glittering pendent in the center around her throat, and teardrop shaped black diamond earrings Tawnyetta had lent her from her Lady MacBrody jewelry stash. With just enough makeup on her eyes to bring out their green even more and a splash of her favorite red lipstick, Sofia was ready to face the evening. Though her insides quivered with anticipation.

At the formal dinner served in the dining room known as Stag Hall, Sofia looked for Ian. He wasn't there. Disappointed, she was able to distract herself by meeting and getting to know Thomas' new girlfriend, Marin.

Marin was pretty enough, light brown hair cut stylishly in a shoulder length do, pale blue eyes that she'd inexplicably done up for the evening with purple and pink eye shadow. Sofia guessed she was trying to match her eggplant colored gown, but the look was not sophisticated. She watched Bridget barely give the poor thing a cursory glance as she flounced past her in her pale pink goddess dress. If there was one thing Bridget couldn't abide, it was poorly done makeup. Especially on the woman who had taken Thomas away from their inner group.

"This is Sofia," Thomas ignored Bridget's rebuff of his girlfriend and focused on introducing her to Sofia.

"Very nice to meet you," Sofia smiled and shook Marin's hand, which seemed frail and cold. She was a little thing and appeared to Sofia to be a bit overwhelmed at this whole Scottish castle experience. Still, Thomas looked happy. And that's all that mattered in the end.

The ballroom looked fantastic. Full of people and gorgeous lighting, Sofia was reminded of the sheer magnificence of this place. Laird and Lady MacBrody made their entrance. Tawnyetta looked so elegant in her strapless black gown that Sofia almost didn't recognize her at first. The beautifully cut bodice showed off her fuller figure, caused by her pregnancy, on top while a wide ruched skirt gave the dress volume and grace. She looked like a Queen in a fairy tale. Under the sections of the skirt that had been lifted and re-attached to give the ruche effect, there were slivers of grey silk peeking through the black. Standing next to Michael in his black and grey tartan kilt and tailored black jacket, they were positively regal.

"Doesn't she look amazing," Bea said what they were all thinking. She and Travis had arrived at the party shortly after Sofia. Sofia nodded in agreement. "And this," Bea touched one of the bird silhouettes on Sofia's skirt. "This is really spec-tacular."

"I'm glad you found it," Sofia answered with a laugh. She felt beautiful in this dress. Stylish and femininely chic. A giddy excitement had come over her at the formal dinner and had filled her completely since entering the ballroom. Anticipation. This was something she normally tried to keep in check, always the realist. This night was different somehow, Sofia thought. She felt different.

The orchestra had started to play. Michael led Tawnyetta to the dance floor and kicked off the festivities with a waltz. As other couples followed suit, Sofia heard the sound of a man clearing his throat. She turned to see Travis, looking a little sick to his stomach, holding his hand gallantly out to his wife.

"Bea?" Travis said, trying to get her attention. He glanced at Sofia with a nervous smile. She gave him a supportive grin then nudged Bea gently.

"Bea, Travis has a question for you," she said, indicating Travis with a nod of her head.

Bea turned and was taken aback by the genteel way her husband was addressing her.

Travis spoke again, this time with more confidence. "May I have this dance?"

"What?" Bea's surprise popped out of her in a high-pitched question. Her gaze flicked around, as if looking for others in on the joke.

Travis cleared his throat again. "May I have this dance, Mrs. Prescott?"

Bea giggled. "Don't be silly," she waved at him as if he was a pesky fly.

Sofia, sensing Travis' determination beginning to wane, stepped in. "He's not joking, Bea. He had dance lessons this afternoon." Bea looked at her with disbelief. "He's quite good," Sofia reassured her.

Watching Travis lead an astonished Bea to the dance floor warmed her heart. It appeared that Henry had already asked Liza as she could see them moving efficiently, if not beautifully, across the floor. Soon she expected to see Professor Shipley and Dr. Clara out there as well. Sofia glanced around. There was still no sign of Ian. The excited buzzing feeling she had been experiencing was beginning to dull.

"Looking for Mr. Wonderful?" Bridget asked. She had approached when Sofia was scanning the room for Ian. Her big blue eyes twinkled with mischief as she sipped a glass of champagne.

"Mr. Who?" Sofia responded innocently.

"Champagne?" Luna joined them, offering Sofia one of the two flutes she held in her hands.

Bridget scoffed lightly, "Or maybe that's not his name." She turned slowly, searching across all of the faces in the ballroom. "He looked more like a Mr. Rebel or Mr. Dangerous to me."

"Who are we talking about?" Angie asked. She, too, had been on a mission to find champagne and returned. She took a sip as she tried to catch up on the conversation.

Sofia gratefully accepted the champagne Luna offered her and took such a big swig that the bubbles went up her nose and made her choke and cough. This, however, was not enough of a distraction to deter Bridget from finding out more about Ian.

"We are talking about the guy with the rock band, Gigi," Bridget said to Angie. "He's tall, lean, ginger like you, with tattoos. Super sexy." She wiggled her eyebrows up and down as her voice changed to a sing-song tone, "And he's a good dancer!"

"Hullo," a man's voice came from behind them.

All four women pivoted to find Ian standing directly behind them.

Eyes wide, Bridget swallowed hard then said, "Hello."

Sofia started to speak, but the choking fit she had experienced just moments ago lingered in her throat and she found herself coughing, eyes watering, and wishing she could escape. But she could barely breathe, let alone escape.

"Are you okay?" Ian stepped forward and took her arm. Sofia tried to shake him off and say she was okay, but the tickle in her throat made her cough even harder.

"Maybe she needs air," Angie suggested.

Ian took hold of her and led her quickly through the crowd, Sofia snorting and choking as they went. He took her onto a side balcony off the ballroom, followed by Angie, Bridget, and Luna. The balcony was decorated with tiny white lights and had a nice view of the formal garden. Sofia was no longer choking, but she allowed herself to be escorted out of the ballroom to avoid the looks their ungraceful exit was receiving.

"I'm fine, really," she insisted as she turned to face Ian. When she got a good look at him in the glow of the white lights her heart skipped a beat. He wore a solid black tuxedo with shining lapels, a black shirt and a black silk tie. His beard had been neatly trimmed, and he smelled amazing. He still wore his silver rings and for some reason she found this detail titillating.

"Do you want some water or something?" Ian's face was full of concern. His hand lingered near her elbow as if ready to catch her should she faint.

"We'll get her some water," Luna said loudly.

"We don't all three–" Bridget began to argue, but Luna interrupted by tugging both Bridget and Angie's arms insistently.

"We'll go find some water and bring it back," Luna called out over her shoulder to Sofia as she quickly led a befuddled Bridget and concerned Angie back into the crowded ballroom.

Ian watched them with a smile then turned his golden eyes to her. "Your friends are funny."

"Yes," Sofia slipped her gaze from him and let it follow the backs of her three friends as they disappeared. At the very last moment, Luna looked back at her. Catching her eye, her cousin smiled excitedly. Sofia knew she'd left her alone with Ian on purpose. "They're the best."

She looked back to Ian. Even dressed to the nines, Ian Law had an edge to him. One that couldn't be erased by formal wear. Muffled sounds of orchestral music came from the closed doors. The damp night air was chilly, but felt good after the warmth of the crowded ballroom. She was thankful for it, actually, because it kept her from overheating due to her pounding heart.

"You look handsome," she said.

He dipped his head, a little bashful, dropping his eyes to the floor, and she was completely charmed. As good looking as he was, and a talented showman as well, Ian had a humble streak at times that was utterly adorable.

He leaned in and lifted his eyes to hers. Those hypnotic golden eyes. "You look amazing," he spoke softly, and the deep tones of his voice were like velvet brushing against her skin. Sofia sucked in her breath as a delicious tickle shimmied across her bare shoulders.

"Thank you," she managed, but it was barely a whisper. No problem. Ian was so close, he heard her perfectly. The corners of his eyes crinkled into a smile and Sofia fought the urge to reach out and touch his beard. She wanted to touch his beard so badly it made her stomach tight.

"I mean...that dress..." he let his eyes drop from hers and move appreciatively over her cheeks and lips, down her throat and to her cleavage that lifted with each breath from underneath her second hand Oscar de la Renta. Sofia silently blessed Bea for finding it at the thrift store. His gaze lingered there and warmth filled her entire body. She wondered if he was fighting the urge to touch her as well. After a few moments when Sofia thought she might burst if he didn't pull her to him and kiss her, Ian shook off whatever thought was holding him and returned his gaze to hers. He glanced around, verifying they were still alone on the patio then looked back to her. "Sofia..." he hesitated.

A few beats went by. She answered, "Yes?"

He took in a breath and blew it out. Clearing his throat nervously, he gathered his courage and said, "I want to talk to you about something."

Chapter Twenty-Two

For one completely insane moment Sofia felt certain he was about to propose. She froze, her smile stuck to her face as her mind raced with that thought. No. That was ridiculous. Impossible. The core of her body trembled at the idea even as she used her inner voice to talk herself down.

After a few drawn out seconds she managed to say, "Okay...what about?"

He leaned toward her, then pulled back, then shoved his hands into his pockets like he didn't know what to do. Even in his stylish tuxedo with his new ultra manly beard, he looked so nervous. Uncertain. It was devastatingly attractive.

"I think..." he hesitated, rethought what he was about to say, then started again, "You and I...us..." He watched for her reaction to the use of that word. She didn't object so he carried on. "I've been thinking that maybe, perhaps, we should rethink this friends only thing."

Sofia opened her mouth to respond. Every piece of her wanted to shout out, "Yes, me too!" But before she could answer, Ian continued. It was as if a faucet had been turned on and the words and emotions he'd been experiencing for the past few months spilled out of his mouth. He confessed them to her with a mixture of relief and trepidation.

"I can't stop thinking about you, Sofia. Since the first time I saw you...here." His eyes moved to the inside of the ballroom where she had first seen him perform and he had singled her out with a wink.

The moment came back to her and she experienced the same electric shock of attraction that she had felt then. It rippled through her body. She nodded in agreement. Not wanting to talk over him, just wanting to hear him say the words and bask in the sound of his voice.

Ian pulled one hand out of his pocket and ran it through his hair, impatient with himself to continue. "I know you think we're too different to be a couple and there's the whole international issue to consider. But it's worked for those two," he gestured toward the patio door and the party where Tawnyetta and Michael were happily presiding over the ball. "I don't know why it couldn't work for us." The easy way he now referred to them as 'us' weakened any of her remaining resistance and a quiet sigh escaped her throat. Sensing that he may be convincing her, he continued passionately, "These past few months have been the most amazing months of my life. And do you know why that is?" He didn't wait for a response. "Because I know that you exist in the world."

Sofia's heart warmed in her chest where it beat so hard and so deep she thought for sure he could hear it pounding. Instinctively, she reached out to him and he took her hand in both of his, surrounding it in the same gentle strength she'd craved since they danced this afternoon.

He moved closer, his voice low and husky. His eyes shone with emotion. "But they've been the worst months of my life as well. It's horrible not seeing you, Sofia. I can't get you out of my heart."

A thousand words swirled through her mind. A thousand ways she could tell him that there was a hole in her life since he'd gone away. That the way she felt when she was with him was not like any other feeling she had ever had in her life. He made her feel light. Relaxed. He made her laugh. He made her feel like the world was one big adventure. She wanted to tell him all of this and more, but the words wouldn't cooperate. They refused to form a coherent sentence and in the end all she could say was, "Ian..."

That was all the encouragement he needed. Ian slipped one hand around her waist, pulling her to him. Her breath caught in her throat. He looked down into her eyes. It was like a magnet pulled her closer and closer to him with an invisible, unbreakable, attraction. She lifted her chin, her mouth was so close to his, her lips warm with desire.

Ian used his grip on her hand and waist to hold her back. A twinkle in his eyes suggested he was thoroughly enjoying this, the excruciating anticipation of their first kiss. The orchestra began a new song. Notes filtered out to them through the closed doors. The Blue Danube. Ian lifted his eyebrows in delight.

His cheek brushed hers as he bent to whisper into her ear. "It's our song, Luv." The light touch of his breath on her neck made her dizzy. Ian lifted their hands into a proper waltz stance and twirled her across the patio.

Sofia wasn't sure that she was on solid ground any longer. As they danced, her feet barely touched the stone patio, she knew that much. Rejuvenated by the cool, damp air, moving under strings of sparkling white lights, she felt light as a feather. Though the ballroom was full near to bursting, it seemed to Sofia that she and Ian were alone in the world, dancing across this ancient patio, preparing to fly off the edge and over the moonlit gardens.

The song was beautiful, the dancing divine, and the anticipation of what would happen after the song tingled over Sofia's skin. She drank Ian in, the look of him, the way it felt to be in his arms, the way he looked at her as they danced. Passion sparked deep inside of her, igniting a lonely place she'd kept hidden away from the world her whole life. A flame rose in Sofia's center, shedding light on a secret truth that she had never admitted to anyone. A desire she had pushed down ever since she was a young girl and decided to become a doctor.

Sofia wanted to fall in love.

Just like in the movies, just like in the story books, a small, private place in her soul wanted desperately to be swept away by an intelligent, funny, handsome man. It was the first time she had ever admitted this desire to herself. And waltzing with Ian was making her think that this deepest unspoken wish of hers may actually be coming true.

Ian's eyes cut away from hers and looked to the patio doors. Every inch of his body stiffened almost imperceptibly. If they hadn't been so close together, so in tune with each other as they danced, Sofia may never have noticed. Within an instant he brought his eyes back to hers, but there was a flicker of something in them that had nothing to do with Sofia. Something dark and frustrated.

She turned her head to see what had captured his attention. Ian led her in a move that seemed sudden and out of rhythm with the way they had been dancing up to this point. The light and airy feeling she had been experiencing darkened and she turned her head toward the patio doors again, straining slightly to get a better view. She didn't see much, because Ian attempted to lead her in the opposite direction. But what she saw was enough.

Gaudy, bright purple, skin tight dress. Spiky white blonde

hair. Hot pink smeared lips sneering at them through the glass doors. These characteristics belonged to only one person Sofia knew. And they belonged to a person Sofia knew could elicit such a strange response from Ian.

Emery.

Chapter Twenty-Three

There are few things in this world as dangerous as a strong woman who has finally opened her heart to love, only to be betrayed. Emery's presence at the ball, at the patio doors, witnessing the moment she and Ian might be falling in love, pierced Sofia's heart. All of the passion she had been feeling curled around itself until it formed a tight, impenetrable ball in the pit of her stomach. Her feet became like lead and their dancing slowed. She needed to hold Ian's shoulder for support, but was sickened by his touch.

"Sofia..." he began.

He knew. She could see in his eyes that he knew he had lost her.

Heat burned the back of her throat. Angry tears welled in her eyes, but she did not blink them away. She leveled an accusing look at him, moving away from him and leaning on the solid stone wall that surrounded the patio instead.

"Are you all right?" He reached for her arm to help steady her, but she pushed it away.

"What is she doing here?" She flicked her eyes from him to Emery then back again.

"It doesn't matter. She's not important."

"Did you bring her?" Anger rose in her voice.

"No," he said firmly. "I did not bring her." Confusion filled Sofia's face and he tried to explain. "Her uncle's in Parliament or something. I'm sure she got an invitation through him. She did not come with me or the band." He cut his hand through the air for definition.

She didn't know what to say, but the pleasant dizziness she'd been feeling while dancing had soured into disorientation. She was lost and leaned even more heavily against the stone wall for support.

"Don't let her ruin everything," he said.

Her eyes shot to his and she saw the pleading in them. The pain. But it was too late, the flickering light that had begun to bloom inside of her was dark again. Boxed up tightly and protected by the knot in her stomach and the fury in her heart.

She pushed past him toward the patio door, intent on getting away from him and the feelings he brought out.

"Don't go–"

The sound of the orchestra and the party drowned him out as Sofia opened the patio doors. Without giving Emery even a cursory glance, she moved as discreetly into the crowd as possible, hoping that her emotional distress was not as obvious to the outside world as it felt from inside. She didn't look back to see if he was following her. It wouldn't matter. There was no convincing her to stay.

She had to leave the ball. She knew there was no way she could make it through more dancing or merry making. And she could not face watching Ian perform after the orchestra. Her heart twisted in her chest at the thought of it. The way he pulled on her soul with his music, it would be too much.

She found Tawnyetta talking to some diplomatic looking men. Her friend's brow creased in concern when she saw Sofia's state.

"What's happened?" Tawnyetta asked.

Sofia dismissed any issue with a quick shake of her head. "Nothing's happened. I don't feel well."

"Oh no! Do you need anything?"

"No, I just need to go to my room and lay down."

"I'll take you," Tawnyetta moved to excuse herself from her guests.

"No, don't do that."

"I'll get Luna." Tawnyetta scanned the crowd for one of the others.

Sofia laid a hand on Tawnyetta's forearm. "No, I'm fine without anyone. I don't want their evening to be ruined because of me."

It took a little extra convincing for Tawnyetta to allow Sofia to leave the ball on her own, but she managed to do it in the end. She was soon rewarded with the dark quiet of their grand castle guest room. Wearily, Sofia pushed her whole body against the heavy door and heard it click shut. She was alone. Utterly alone.

That's when the tears came, silent and strong. So strong she doubled over and clutched her stomach as she wept. She was shaken to her core, the emotional extremes she'd been feeling were too much. She made it to the bed and collapsed onto it, sobbing into her pillow. By the time Luna checked on her a while later, Sofia had stripped off her gown and curled up tightly under the heavy covers where she slept fitfully into the night.

"You look exhausted," Bridget said as she peered at Sofia over the rim of a crystal cup.

"Gee, thanks," Sofia responded, taking a sip out of her own crystal cup.

Their cups were part of a larger punchbowl set that was currently full of a fizzing pink concoction and set on a buffet table laden with a variety of goodies. Hot flaky cheese puffs, tiny strawberry tarts folded like little diapers, deviled eggs sprinkled with crispy bacon bits, and miniature pink and turquoise cupcakes with tiny white marzipan baby booties on each one were some of the treats. Everything had been created by the castle cook under the guidance of Bridget, who was officially throwing Tawnyetta's baby shower. And officially giving Sofia the third degree.

"I didn't mean it like that," Bridget said.

They had just finished setting up the gift table with balloons and flowers and were taking a minute to taste test the punch before everybody, including the guest of honor, arrived.

"What did you mean it like, then?" Sofia asked. She was feeling sharp and moody. Luna had let her sleep through breakfast, but Bridget had taken that to mean she had plenty of rest and could help her put the final touches on the party.

"I mean I want to know all of the details of what is going on with you and Ian Law," Bridget said, stressing Ian's name.

Sofia cringed internally. "There's nothing going on."

Bridget arched an eyebrow. "Really? Because last we saw you two last night you were thick as thieves on the patio. Then you disappeared."

Sofia had not had time to process everything with Ian since last night. She certainly didn't want to do it right now, minutes before they were surrounded by baby shower guests. She shook her head, denying whatever Bridget had concocted in her overactive imagination.

"Nothing happened. I told you. I didn't feel well and I went back to the room and fell asleep."

Bridget studied Sofia's face then shrugged. "If you don't want to tell me, that's fine."

Sofia sighed and wished everyone else would arrive.

Bridget needed a distraction and nothing distracted her quiet so well as a party to command.

The guest list for this party was fairly short, even though Bridget had announced it as a co-ed party. Michael would accompany Tawnyetta, of course. Luna and Angie should be there soon. Bea and Travis had promised to come. Thomas would be here with Marin, because where else would she go? Even though she barely knew Tawnyetta, she was Thomas' girlfriend and went with him everywhere according to Luna and Angie. Sofia wondered what that would be like, to have someone you loved with you at all of your important events. A fresh wave of sadness washed over her.

"Welcome," Bridget said with delight as Liza poked her head into the room. Bridget had invited Liza and Dr. Clara as they were Sofia's guests. Henry also came, mostly because he was following Liza around.

In a short time the small parlor style room was full of happy, chatting people. Sofia did her best to fit in. She decided to talk to her three co-workers in order to avoid any more intimate questions from her closer friends.

"Lady MacBrody certainly is a beauty, isn't she?" Dr. Clara commented as she placed three small cupcakes on a china plate.

Sofia smiled. "She is." Tawnyetta was a ball of glowing prettiness at her baby shower. At around five months along she had that radiant mid-pregnancy look about her, especially in the charming maxi dress she'd chosen for the occasion. With black and white stripes on top and a floral print on the bottom she was casual chic and the picture of darling maternity wear.

Sofia glanced down at her own denim dress. It was soft and comfortable, which is why she'd chosen it today. Plus she thought it had that pseudo 70's look that she often saw Meghan Markle wear. She figured if it was stylish enough for the Duchess of Sussex, it would be stylish enough for Lady MacBrody's baby shower.

"And he's a handsome devil, wouldn't you say?" Dr. Clara's beady eyes had shifted and were resting on Michael who had just entered the room. "Can you imagine how attractive their wee bairn will be?" She popped one of the turquoise blue cupcakes whole into her mouth and chuckled with pleasure.

"He is quite handsome," Liza agreed.

Henry puffed up a bit at her comment. "Oh, I don't know. His mouth is a little crooked...if you ask me." All three women looked at him. "I'm just sayin'..." Henry shuffled uncomfortably under their scrutiny and he glared in Michael's general direction. Suddenly, his eyes lit up. "What's this?"

All three women followed his gaze and Sofia felt her heart drop when she saw what Henry had seen. Ian. Walking in the doorway, apparently following Michael, Ian in jeans, a tight black T-shirt, and dark sunglasses, looked every bit the rock star.

"That's Ian Law from The Tellers," Henry exclaimed. If Ian heard him, he didn't respond.

Bea had materialized at Sofia's elbow and corrected Henry, "The Robot Tellers."

Liza furrowed her brow, studying Ian from across the room. She looked at Sofia then back to Ian again. "Isn't he–"

"He was brilliant last night," Henry continued. Ian had definitely found a fan in their young friend. "Did you catch that last song?"

Liza continued to look at Sofia. "I thought he was your–"

"Cupcake?" Bridget appeared in front of them with a tray of goodies.

Dr. Clara took another blue cupcake as she said, "Yes, yes, Liza. I thought he was, too."

"Thought who was what?" Bridget asked.

"Ian Law," Henry explained. He pointed at Ian as he said it and this time Sofia was sure Ian had heard him, because he turned to look at them. "He's the lead singer of The Tellers."

"The Robot Tellers," Bea corrected again, taking her own pink cupcake from Bridget's tray.

"No, no, no," Dr. Clara chimed in, her deep voice lifting over all the other conversations in the room.

Sofia was frozen where she stood. Her heart beat wildly as she watched Ian take off his sunglasses, his golden eyes locked on hers. Bridget watched them both with rising interest.

"Liza and I were discussing that we've seen him before last night," Dr. Clara explained, so loudly Sofia knew the whole room could hear.

"You've seen him in concert?" Henry asked. Dear, single minded Henry.

Dr. Clara shook her head 'no'. "Actually, we saw him at work when he came to see you." She turned to Sofia with an amused smile and, her voice booming, said, "We thought he was your boyfriend!"

Chapter Twenty-Four

The room fell into an awkward silence as all eyes turned to Sofia. Ian lifted his eyebrows in amused surprise and kept his eyes locked on hers. As heat rose in her cheeks Sofia tore her gaze away from Ian and searched the room for any reason that she could leave. On the buffet table she spied the almost empty cheese puff tray.

"Cheese puffs," she said. Mild confusion flickered across everyone's faces. Especially Ian's. "We're almost out of cheese puffs. I'll go check on that."

"We can ring for–" Bridget started to explain that there were servants to help them with things like cheese puffs.

"I'll check on it," Sofia insisted. She grabbed the almost empty tray and made her escape out the door. In her haste to leave she moved the tray so swiftly that two cheese puffs rolled off and bounced onto the ornate rug. Sofia was so embarrassed she didn't stop to pick them up.

Hurrying through the Great Hall toward the kitchen, Sofia heard Luna's voice calling to her to wait.

"I'll be right back," Sofia said over her shoulder as she

continued at a full speed walk to the kitchen. By the time she reached the door Luna had caught up.

"Sofia, what's going on?" Luna tried to get her cousin to focus.

"I'm getting cheese puffs."

"No, you're not. You're running away. What happened with Ian last night?"

"Yoo-hoo!" Bridget called out. She and Angie were now at the end of the hall, hurrying in Sofia and Luna's direction. "Wait up!"

Sofia let out a frustrated sigh and shoved the kitchen door open, almost knocking it into the maid, Anne, who was exiting the kitchen. After many apologies to the kitchen staff, Luna steered Sofia and her tray of cheese puffs into the empty dining hall next to the kitchen. They were joined almost immediately by Bridget and Angie.

"You can't fool us, Fifi. Something is going on," Bridget said.

"Is that gorgeous singer your boyfriend?" Angie asked, both delighted and impressed.

"No," Sofia denied it, but she had to fight the urge to smile.

"Aha!" Bridget pointed her French manicured finger at Sofia. "He is, isn't he? I knew it!"

"He's not my boyfriend, Bridget," Sofia retorted. Even the word 'boyfriend' felt strange coming out of her mouth.

"What is he then?" Luna asked.

"What am I missing?" Tawnyetta asked as she came in the room. She was hurrying, though her normal athletic gate was more of an athletic waddle because of her swollen belly.

"Sofia may or may not have a boyfriend," Angie told her.

Tawnyetta's eyes flew open in surprise and she stopped in her tracks. "Ian? Oh, Sofia! He's such a cool guy."

"Yeah, he's really attractive...in a grunge rock kind of way,"

Angie said. "And I'm not just saying that because he's a fellow ginger."

Sofia felt a little queasy and she couldn't tell if it was from excitement at her friend's enthusiasm or embarrassment at the whole mess with Ian coming under their scrutiny.

"Maybe we should let her talk," Luna suggested. She had been keeping a cautious eye on her cousin and could probably tell she was in a state.

The friends fell obediently in line. They pulled dining room chairs up in a cluster surrounding Sofia and waited, some more patiently than others. Sofia took a few deep breaths and thought about how to explain everything to her best friends. She finally decided to start at the beginning, when Ian had taken her on their first date to eat fish n' chips and ride The London Eye, and how she'd felt confused and disrupted ever since. She opened her mouth to speak and Thomas poked his head into the room.

"Sooo...you guys realize there's almost nobody left at the party, right?" He quipped. Then he noticed the support circle that was happening and his brow knit together. "What's wrong?"

"Sofia's about to tell us about her and Ian," Bridget said in her most scolding tone. "Come sit down and be quiet."

Thomas lifted his eyebrows as he grabbed a chair and set it next to Sofia. He plunked down in the chair and leaned his shoulder into hers. "Ian?" He nodded with approval. "He seems like a good match."

Sofia's face screwed up with skepticism. "He is not a good match for me."

"Oh," Thomas stood corrected. He waited a few beats until curiosity overtook him, then asked, "And why is that?"

Scoffing heartily, Sofia explained, "He sings in a rock band. That's his job. He doesn't have a real job. He doesn't have a career." Her friend's blank faces stared at her, not seeming to understand. "And he's kind of loose and artsy, you know? What about those tattoos? My father would die of a heart attack if I brought home a man with all of those tattoos."

Her commentary was met with complete silence except for Luna and Tawnyetta who exchanged an amused glanced.

"What is that look for?" Sofia asked, her eyes cutting between Luna and Tawnyetta suspiciously.

"It's nothing," Tawnyetta said.

Sofia glared at them until Luna caved and answered, "It's just that your Dad is not going to like anybody you bring home, Sofia. He's kind of old fashioned that way."

They had a point, Sofia had to admit. She sighed heavily and drummed her nails on the table top. Finally she threw up one hand and said, "He's just not my type."

"Really?" Bridget obviously didn't believe her. "Sexy rock star doesn't do it for you?"

Thomas turned his attention to Bridget, shrugging a little, "Is he that sexy? Honestly?" She nodded knowingly and all of the others, minus Sofia, joined in. Thomas seemed put out. He shrugged again and looked down at his hands, mumbling, "His eyes are kind of weird."

Sofia bristled a little at the comment. "They're not weird," she said. Then, more quietly, "I like his eyes."

Bridget pointed at her, "See? You like him."

Sofia sighed. Sometimes Bridget really annoyed her. Especially when she was right.

Angie, their group counselor, chimed in, "Why don't you want to like him? That's the real question."

It was a question that wouldn't be answered immediately. Michael arrived looking worried and Tawnyetta had to excuse herself back to her baby shower. Bridget, as the host of the party, went with her. Sofia felt guilty for disrupting her friend's big day.

"Come on, it doesn't matter right now. Let's get back to

the party and watch Tawnyetta open presents," she told the others.

Any concerns she had of having to face Ian at the baby shower were unfounded, as he had left while she was gone. Free to enjoy this time with her friends and celebrate the upcoming birth of the little Laird or Lady, Sofia did her best to bring up her mood.

She sipped punch and played silly games and offered name suggestions for the unborn child. As she did all of these things she became more and more aware of a shift in her feelings.

Watching the way Michael looked at Tawnyetta, the way her touched her hair when he spoke to her, and leaned in to listen to every word that came out of her mouth was like watching a beautiful dance. A dance between two lovers, two friends. The whole scene seemed to magnify her solo status and the lonely ache that had taken up seemingly permanent residence in her heart.

Sofia watched Bridget as she cooed and fawned over Tawnyetta, treating her as much like a queen for the day as they all knew Bridget herself wanted to be treated. Bridget took so much care to ensure her friend had the most perfect experience at her baby shower, because that's what Bridget did. She tried to give them all princess treatment. Even when she was being intrusive and bossy about their love lives, she did have a keen eye for romance. Bridget was almost always right about matters of the heart. Except when it came to her own love life, ironically. As much as Sofia hated to admit it, Bridget was right about her and Ian.

She did like Ian. She more than liked him. Being here with all of her friends, and witnessing Tawnyetta and Michael's domestic bliss, brought this fact more sharply into focus. Once again the hollow feeling in her heart told her that she was missing something. Missing him. She missed him being next to her, touching her, trying to pull her out of her shell, trying to make her laugh. Her heart echoed with longing and she thought she might sink into tears again.

"Have you made up your mind?" Angie asked. She had sidled up next to Sofia at the buffet table.

"Made up my mind?"

Angie nodded, her glorious red tresses bobbing up and down as she did. "You know, about Ian." Sofia blinked in surprise. Angie was reading her mind.

Oddly, Sofia realized that she did, in fact, have an answer to the question. "Yes, I have made up my mind," she said with a confidence that surprised her.

Angie grinned, because she already knew what Sofia had decided. She was going to go for it. As soon as the festivities were over she would find Ian and tell him how she felt. They could work through whatever issue she had with Emery. She could learn to live with his lack of a career. Why should she throw away someone who had touched her heart the way Ian Law had touched hers?

After the party was over and they all went to their respective rooms to rest up and get packed for the trip back to London, Sofia took a few minutes to freshen up for her big conversation with Ian.

"Were you going to tell me?" Luna asked from the doorway to their shared bathroom.

Sofia was pulling a brush through her long, dark hair, leaving it soft and shiny. "Tell you?"

"Angie said you're going to go for it with Ian...and you haven't even told me yet!"

Butterflies erupted in Sofia's stomach at hearing those words. Having her friends involved made the whole thing more real. This was probably why she'd avoided talking to them about Ian earlier. She put the brush down and turned to her cousin.

"It's because I'm so nervous and excited," she said in the

high-pitched tone of a teenager. Luna gave her a delighted hug. "Now I just need to find him in this huge place," Sofia added.

With just hours remaining before she was supposed to drive back to Inverness to catch the overnight train, Sofia scoured the public areas of the castle looking for Ian. The day was cold and dreary and she didn't think he would be in the gardens, but she couldn't find him anywhere inside either. At one point she thought she was on the right track when she went to the ballroom. Maybe he was packing up his gear with the band. But the ballroom was nothing more than a huge, cold, empty space. A shadow of what it had been last night full of light and music and people.

She stood in the echoing space and shivered. Rainy day afternoon light filled the tall windows and injected a sense of doom into her little mission. Trickles of doubt ran through her, making her hug herself to stave off another shiver. Where was he? In his room, maybe? She'd have to find out what room he was in. How would she go about doing that?

Sofia had another idea. What about the kitchen? She hadn't checked in there yet, as it was usually full of staff, not guests. But if he wasn't in the kitchen at least she might be able to find out from one of the staff members what room he was in.

Bolstered by this new plan of action, Sofia turned on her heel and left the cold ballroom for the warm and welcoming kitchen. Her heart was still hopeful, but a fear of failure had started to needle the back of her mind. She needed to find Ian, and find him soon, or she was afraid the fragile confidence she had in her decision would begin to crack.

Chapter Twenty-Five

S he did not find Ian in the kitchen. What she did find was a bustle of activity as the staff prepared one of their famous elaborate dinners for the castle guests. And she found Michael, who had come to the kitchen specifically to get pickled herring and strawberries for his wife. Apparently Tawnyetta was having a pregnancy craving.

"Can I help you with anything?" Michael asked. His Scottish brogue added charm to everything he said.

Sofia answered, "Yes." Then she hesitated. Knowing that Ian was one of Michael's good friends, she wanted to choose her words carefully. She cleared her throat. "I was actually...I thought maybe...." Finally, she spit it out, "I'm looking for Ian."

Understanding flickered through Michael's eyes, and the corners of his mouth lifted into an almost smile. She had not considered the fact that since he and Ian were friends, Ian may have shared her ridiculous behavior with him. Their on again, off again, somewhat of a romance may be old news to Michael. As she looked into his deep blue eyes, she thought she could sense that he knew the truth. To his credit, Michael didn't say anything. Ever the gentleman. Thank goodness. Sofia's cheeks turned beet red. He recognized her embarrassment and the warm amusement on his face shifted to polite concern. "I'm afraid he's already left. They left a few hours ago."

Sofia's stomach sank. "Back to London?" Of course, that was a stupid question. Thankfully, Michael did not chastise her for it, though the compassion in his eyes bordered on pity, which made her feel even more stupid.

"Yes, I believe so."

"Thank you," she managed as she turned to leave, unable to continue talking while her stomach roiled with deep disappointment.

"Sofia," Michael stopped her and she looked back at him. "Have you tried calling him?"

She stood numbly, astounded at her own absurdity. No. She hadn't. That would be something a normal person would do. She mumbled a thank you and said something like, "I'll try that," before escaping out the door.

She retreated to the only place she had been that day that had been completely deserted. The ballroom. She leaned against the wall, pulling her phone from her pocket...and staring at it.

She couldn't believe she hadn't thought to call Ian before Michael mentioned it. Okay, everything was still going to be just fine. She would call. No, texting would be better. Less weird. She tried to brush off the mistake and focus on her phone again. Her fingers poised over the glowing screen, but didn't move. Like someone frozen in time she stood there gaping at her phone, drawing a complete blank.

What should she say?

"Ugh!" Throwing her head back she grimaced at the ceiling. "This is impossible."

Her phone buzzed in her hand and she looked swiftly

down, hoping against hope that Ian had beat her to the whole texting thing.

We're getting ready to load the car. Where are you?

It wasn't a text from Ian, it was from Luna. And it was time to go.

"Can't sleep?" Thomas asked.

Sofia jerked at the sound of his voice. She had been virtually alone in the lounge car since she got out of she and Luna's tiny berth. She'd found a spot on an empty long couch almost an hour ago and was nursing a whiskey sour, staring at her phone.

She shook her head 'no'. "You?"

As an answer Thomas plopped down by her and ran his hand through his hair, making it stick out in all directions. He let out a heavy sigh. He looked tired. Maybe riding a train all night was taking its toll on him. Or maybe it was traveling with Marin.

Sofia sensed that even though Thomas seemed very much attached to Marin, all of the togetherness of the past few days was getting to him. It wasn't like they were on a romantic getaway alone. They were almost constantly with his oldest friends, who also happened to be a group of girls. The entire group, minus Tawnyetta and Michael, had decided to go back to London with Sofia and hang out for a few more days together. And even though most of them, minus Bridget, were polite and welcoming to Marin, she kind of didn't fit in.

The lounge car attendant took Thomas' order. "I'll have what she's having," Thomas told the man. He sat back in the couch and flicked a look at her phone. "You waiting for a call?"

Again, Sofia shook her head 'no'. "Not exactly."

He pushed his bottom lip out as he nodded, considering

her answer. "It's after midnight, you're sitting alone drinking and staring at your phone, but you're not expecting a call." Sofia raised her eyebrow at him, waiting for the sarcasm. He snapped his fingers and pointed at her. "I've got it. You're drunk texting."

She chuckled. "No...not exactly."

That was the truth. She had not texted Ian since she decided to earlier in the day, she was still thinking about what to say, and she was drinking a whisky sour. So, technically, Thomas was half correct.

"It's that rock star with the weird eyes, isn't it?"

"He doesn't have weird eyes!"

Thomas nodded knowingly, "I knew it."

She pushed on his knee, "What about you? Why aren't you with Marin?"

Thomas slumped down in the couch and dropped his head back so it rested on the top cushion. He let out a groan of frustration and said to the ceiling, "She snores."

Sofia couldn't suppress a giggle before saying, "No, she doesn't."

"Oh, yes, she does," he said with such seriousness it made Sofia laugh out loud. "It's not funny. I have barely slept this whole trip." Sofia laughed even harder. He turned to look at her without lifting his head off of the cushion. "Let's get back to you and ol' crazy eyes."

"You're impossible."

"What are you texting him?" Thomas reached for her phone. She pulled her arm back so he couldn't take it.

"Nothing, yet." It was her turn to slump down into the couch. "I don't know what to say."

"How far into this thing are you with this guy?"

"We've been on a few dates when I first moved here. Then we decided to be friends. But we danced a few times at the castle and...now I'm not sure."

"Ah, the dreaded 'friends'." Thomas used his fingers to make air quotes when he said 'friends'. "That sucks."

From his tone it sounded like Thomas had personal experience with the issue. Sofia tried to remember a time that he had been stuck as 'friends' when he really wanted something else. Nothing came to mind.

Her eyebrows knit together in confusion. "You speak from experience?"

The lounge car attendant arrived with his drink and Thomas made a big show of paying the man and tipping him. Then he took a big gulp as if he was dying of thirst. Sofia watched him with narrowed eyes, but when she started to ask him again, he changed the subject.

"Let me ask you this, Sofia. Who was the one who decided you should be friends?"

The question stopped her thought process and brought her crashing back down to her reality. She shrugged, not wanting to admit it had been her who suggested–or demanded–that they remain friends.

Thomas gave her a look and she admitted with a sigh, "I did."

"Why does this not surprise me?"

"I have a lot going on these days," she said meekly.

He nodded toward her cell phone. "And now you feel differently?"

"Yes," her voice cracked a little bit as her emotions tried to surface. Thomas watched her evenly as she swallowed hard and put on a brave face.

He gave her his most supportive brotherly expression and said, "You know, you can be a doctor–sorry, a professor–and still have a love life. People do it all the time. Every day on every continent."

A small piece of the wall around her heart crumbled at his words. Hot tears pressed at the back of her throat and kept her from speaking. But when she looked at Thomas, she knew that he could see them there.

"You really like him?" he asked.

She nodded and looked down at her hands. She had to bite her bottom lip to stop herself from crying. Her fingers trembled around her cell phone and she let it drop into her lap in dismay.

"Then text him," he urged her. Then, realizing that she was torn, he teased, "Or, better yet, I'll text him for you." Thomas pulled out his phone. "That way you don't have to be vulnerable."

"No, don't," she laughed a little bit.

"Why not? It's only..." he looked at his phone, "One o'clock in the morning. He's a rock star, he probably stays up all night anyway."

She smiled again. "It's too late to text him now. It would be weird. Plus, you don't have his number."

He fell back, defeated. But he had made her smile, which was a victory in the end.

"All right," he said. "Promise you will talk to him when we get to London? I don't like seeing you upset like this."

Thomas, her dear friend, she smiled at him. "I will," she promised.

And in that moment Sofia absolutely meant it.

Chapter Twenty-Six

Getting home early in the morning after a cramped and, for some of them, sleepless night on the train was hard on the whole group. Angie and Luna looked tousled and unkempt like little children who had been woken up too early. Liza and Henry wore their rumpled grad student looks complete with oversized, faded sweatshirts from King's College. Professor Shipley and Thomas both glowered at the world, hardly communicating with anything more than a bear like grumble. Bridget wore lack of sleep like a movie star, unrelentingly beautiful in yoga pants, a loose grey T-shirt and her blonde tresses up in a stylish messy bun. Dr. Clara and Marin, opposites in every way physically, were the only two of their crew that were in good spirits. Watching Thomas wearily carry both he and Marin's luggage off the train as Marin chattered happily away with Dr. Clara was mildly entertaining for Sofia, especially since she knew how Marin's snoring had kept him awake.

Sofia was exhausted on every level. Getting back to her flat with Luna while the others went to their homes or hotels was a daunting task. Once home, she crawled into bed and slept for hours. Not knowing or caring what everyone else was up to, she let her fatigue numb any thought of Ian. When she woke up, the drive to contact him had faded into something else–a soreness in her heart, but one that she thought she could ignore for a little while longer. Who knew? Maybe it would fade over time.

There was the complete pandemonium of returning home with so much company in town to focus on. Going back to work after a long weekend was also a good distraction. All of these were solid reasons in Sofia's mind to postpone the inevitable text. The longer she waited, the more what had been a good idea in the middle of the night on the train talking to Thomas seemed silly, almost childish. So much so, that she chose to spend the next few days diving into her work at the university and losing herself in frivolous outings with her friends each evening.

"It's opening night for Jonas Novak at the Peckham Gallery," Bea told them at the large table they were sharing in a stylish Turkish restaurant. "It's his first exhibit in London ever." She and Travis were inviting all of their American friends to see a hot contemporary painter from Prague. "You have to come," she encouraged them, her bright eyes dancing with the excitement of it all.

"Of course we're coming," Bridget answered for everyone. "It's our last night here, we have to do something fabulous." Her confidence in the group's agreement was unshakeable after years of leading their social engagements. Not even Marin, watching the conversation over a plate of quail kebabs, dared object.

With an almost imperceptible glance at Sofia, Bridget asked Bea, "Will Ian be joining us?"

Sofia stopped chewing. A hesitant hush fell over the whole table. All except for Marin who was noisily sucking on a tiny quail bone.

Though she was astonished at Bridget's pushy question, Sofia didn't look up. She concentrated on her food and pretended she hadn't heard it. The rest of the group followed her lead. None of them were sure what Bridget was up to, so they all stayed quiet. Except Bea. Whether because of nerves or oblivious to the uncomfortable silence, Bea chattered away.

"No, actually," Bea said. "I asked him, because he's so much fun at these things. But he couldn't. He's playing a concert tonight." Relief flooded Sofia and the strange vibe in the air lifted. Bea continued, "It's actually on the same street as the art exhibit. The place is named Higher Calling. It used to be a derelict chapel that they renovated into a music venue. Absolutely hectic." She looked around the table for a reaction. When none of them responded, she translated to American for them, "Hip and cool."

The exhibit was unique. Probably brilliant. The artist had used vibrant blues and whites and yellows, slashes and smears, and undulating wave form shapes. The paint spilled off the canvas, over the frame and onto the walls of the gallery, creating what looked like an ocean of interpretive color. Everyone agreed it was one of the most intriguing art exhibits they'd ever seen.

Sofia wished she could enjoy it. Her head had been spinning ever since Bridget brought up Ian's name at dinner. Knowing that he was close by performing at Higher Calling made Sofia's stomach jump whenever a man his height and build appeared in her peripheral vision. She tried to shake it off, the knowledge that he was so close. Her mind wouldn't let go of the possibility that he may walk in at any moment.

That was ridiculous. He was putting on a concert. He was busy. Besides, why would he? She hadn't spoken to him since she left him on the patio during the ball.

Bridget's laughter tumbled through the low murmur of the crowd and Sofia looked in her direction. Why did she have to bring him up in conversation that way? Sofia had been perfectly fine drinking wine and dining out with her friends. She didn't need to be reminded of the whole mess with Ian. It had been callous and insensitive of Bridget, and Sofia was feeling irritated at her.

The spinning in her head whirled a little faster as her annoyance grew. She glanced down at her almost empty wine glass. She'd been drinking a lot of wine this evening. Maybe that was part of her head spinning...and her flailing emotions.

"Love this look, by the way," Bridget had snuck up on her while she was peering into her wine glass. Sofia was wearing a short velvet wraparound dress in hunter green with black suede boots that ended just above her knees. Bridget tugged on the sleeve teasingly. "It's kinda racy."

"Thanks," Sofia said.

"What do you think of this place?" Bridget asked.

Sofia scowled. "It's nice," she punctuated the statement with a sniff.

"What is the matter?"

"You know what," Sofia answered in a huff. Bridget grinned. She did know, she just thought it was funny. Sofia grew more irritated, "What was all that about Ian?"

Bridget's beautifully shaped eyebrows lifted in mock surprise. "Why, Sofia, whatever do you mean?" She was using her fake southern accent, which meant she thought she was being extra charming and sly.

"It wasn't nice of you to embarrass me like that at dinner," Sofia said.

Bridget's expression turned contrite. "I didn't mean it to embarrass you, Fifi." Sofia scoffed. "I didn't!" Bridget looked sincere enough, bothered that Sofia could think she would do anything to hurt her.

Sofia succumbed to her friend's annoying charm. "Then why did you say it?"

Bridget leveled a serious gaze out of her baby blues. So serious that Sofia sobered up as she waited for the answer. When she did respond, Bridget's words hit her hard. "Because I don't want to leave one of my best friends in the world heart broken in London when we fly home tomorrow. You forget, Fifi, I was there when you first saw each other...at Tawny's wedding. I could see it then and I saw it the other night at the ball. I think you're making a big mistake if you push this one away. Maybe the mistake of your life."

Unprepared for this response, Sofia grew silent. The irritation that had been bubbling inside of her since dinner receded and left her slightly bewildered. How much of her feelings for Ian had been so obvious to Bridget and the others? How much of Ian's feelings for her had they witnessed and felt were strong enough to warrant this heavy duty advice?

Bridget was a lot of things, but she wasn't cruel. They had been friends since childhood and there was no way Bridget would send her on a wild goose chase in love. If anything, she was probably more protective of the hearts of her friends than she was her own.

Sofia's silence remained as the evening progressed. She looked at the artwork, listened to the conversations around her, and went to the bar to get another glass of wine. She didn't know how many glasses she had already drank over the course of the evening. She was confused over all of the emotions that were circling through her body. And she wasn't sure how she ended up outside the art gallery staring at a derelict chapel that pulsed with strobe lights and a throbbing bass emanating from its open front doors—the "absolutely hectic" music venue that could only be Higher Calling.

Chapter Twenty-Seven

Cold night air surrounded her, but it felt good after the warm stuffiness of the art gallery. Her black suede boots crunched as she walked on loose pieces of gravel that had come up from between the stones of the sidewalk. She briefly considered going back and getting her jacket, but decided against it. She didn't want to see anyone or have to explain what she was about to do.

People filled the sidewalk and all of the doorways of every building on the narrow street. There were several other art galleries and restaurants on this block in addition to the chapel turned bar. The night was clear, no rain, but a damp chill in the air stayed as a reminder that this was London.

Sofia tore her gaze away from Higher Calling and took in the crowded sidewalk. Groups of friends, lovers, young and old, talked and laughed as they moved from one destination to the next. Lively. Vibrant. Exciting.

The door of Higher Calling was packed. A line of people waiting to get in, even at this late hour, snaked out the front and down the side of the building. They made it impossible for Sofia to get to the large, bald, heavy set bouncer who stood directly at the entrance like a wall of muscle between the people waiting and the lucky ones inside.

She paused at the bottom of the steps leading to the chapel doors, looking up and allowing the music–and the sound of Ian's voice singing–to wash over her. At times deep and growling, at times lifting into a high treble, somewhere between a shout and a scream, rising and falling with the music, louder, softer, his voice pulled everyone, especially Sofia, into its web.

Lights spilled from the door, stretching out over the line of fans and sweeping across the street. They moved over Sofia and she thought she could feel them on her skin. Feel *him*. She closed her eyes and let the sensation take over, not paying any attention to how long she stayed that way.

"Unbelievable." A familiar voice sounded at her elbow.

Sofia's eyes opened to find Emery standing next to her. Wearing a bright white jacket that looked like it had been made out of a shag carpet and matched her spiky hair, she was chewing pink gum instead of smoking her regular cigarette, and glowering at Sofia.

"I came to see him," Sofia said calmly. Surprised that Emery's presence didn't incite jealousy or anger in her, Sofia lifted one shoulder in a little shrug and said, "But I don't have a ticket."

Emery stared at her for a few moments, chewing the wad of gum in her mouth thoughtfully. She, too, seemed surprised at Sofia's reaction. She blew a bubble, letting it snap and pulling it back into her mouth with her tongue. Her eyes shifted to the line of fans waiting to get in, then to the bouncer, then back to Sofia. She scrunched her nose up like a child considering their options. Apparently landing on the best move, Emery let out a heavy sigh and her normally combative stance flopped in on itself so she looked comically deflated.

With a roll of her eyes she muttered in a disgruntled tone,

"He will kill me if I don't help you." She reluctantly reached out to Sofia and said, "Come on."

Emery pulled her up the steps and, after a few words with the burly bouncer, through the front doors of Higher Calling raising a few complaints from the line of fans. Emery ignored them. In fact, she mostly ignored Sofia, too, who continued following her only because she didn't know what else to do. Even if she wanted to ask Emery where she was taking her, she couldn't have over the music. Now surrounding them, the pounding of the song vibrated through Sofia's whole body. Ian's song rose around her, wrapping her in its rhythm, numbing her to anything else.

Instead of taking her to the front of the pulsating crowd, Emery led Sofia down the side of the venue and through a heavy door that must have once been used by deacons or alter boys during church services. Flashes of the impressive architecture over the stage lit by purple and red lights imprinted on Sofia's mind as she disappeared with Emery into the back hallway.

"You can wait for him back here," Emery said over her shoulder. The sounds of the concert were muffled in the hallway, but not gone. As the current song ended, the din of a cheering crowd rose on the other side of the wall. They came to a door and Emery shoved it open, revealing a well lit room with two couches and a familiar snack filled card table at one end. Emery deposited Sofia alone in the room and left with only a cursory acceptance of her thanks.

With the concert now only a distant thumping, and nobody around to distract her, Sofia's nerves rushed through her. She had not started out toward Higher Calling with much of a plan, but this wasn't what she had expected.

"What did you expect?" she asked out loud. There was nobody there to answer.

By the time the concert was over, Sofia had second guessed

her decision to leave the art gallery, look for Ian, follow Emery, and allow herself to be stuck in this little room without any idea what was going to happen next. For all she knew, Emery could have hid her away in here until Ian left the building. Or even locked the door so Sofia couldn't leave. She tried the knob just to be sure and it turned. With relief, she pulled the door open, but saw only a dimly lit hallway with nobody in sight.

After a few more minutes of self-doubt, Sofia decided this was probably a big mistake. There were other ways she could get in touch with Ian. She didn't have to secretly hide out backstage at his concert. She went to the door again and grabbed the knob. At the same moment that she pulled someone else pushed from the other side and the door flung open into Ian's surprised face.

If he was shocked to see her, Sofia was even more shocked to see him in his current state. Hot and sweaty from performing, it appeared Ian had taken his shirt off when he got backstage. He stood bare chested in front of her, with tattoos twisting across his muscled arms, chest, and abs. Wearing only faded jeans and black boots, he was still revved up from the concert and his cat eyes flashed.

Sofia swallowed. Hard.

"Hullo," he said, his voice raspy from use.

"Hi," she answered.

He glanced behind her into the empty room. "May I?"

"Of course," she blushed a little and stepped back to let him in. Not quickly enough to avoid his bare skin brushing against her as he did. A thrill jolted to the center of her body as they touched.

Ian tossed his shirt on the couch and went to the snack table. Her eyes wandered across his wide shoulders that tapered perfectly into a lean waist. Her gaze rested with curiosity on the tattoo that stretched down the length of his spine from just above his shoulder blades to where it ended at the waistband of his jeans. In the shape of a guitar, the tattoo was only made up of black ink. But it wasn't actually a guitar. It was the silhouette of trees on a lake on one half and their reflection making up the other half. Mirrored images of a landscape, but in the shape of a guitar. The whole image was intriguing. Especially on Ian's naked back. Her lips parted as she followed the lines of his body. The sight of him literally took her breath away.

"Emery said I had a surprise down here," he said as he grabbed a bottle of water and twisted off the lid, turning back around to look at her. "She meant you?"

Sofia nodded self-consciously. "I guess so."

He drank from the bottle, never taking his eyes off of her, and Sofia felt almost as exposed as he looked. He gestured toward the cart in a silent offer. She nodded. He picked up another bottle of water and brought it to her. Sofia could barely keep her eyes on his, she was distracted by the ridges of his six-pack abs and the way his jeans hung low on his hips.

"And to what do I owe this pleasure?" he asked as she took the bottle of water from his hand.

"I was next door," Sofia explained. "Bea said you were here. Emery got me in." He took another swig and waited. "I wanted to..." she searched for the right words, but only came up with, "say hi." Ian's eyebrows lifted and she was compelled to explain more. "After we danced...I was going to call or text or something–"

"Why didn't you?"

She didn't have an answer to that question. And after a few moments, Ian knew it. He shook his head and looked away into the empty space between her and the door. When he returned his eyes to hers, the look in them cut into her heart like ice. Ian stepped away and sat on the armrest of the nearest couch facing her. He had his feet kicked out in front of him and his arms crossed over his chest, regarding her with a skeptical expression that stung.

"I didn't know what to say..." her words came out half choked.

Again, he shook his head and looked away. He let out a sharp laugh and said, "I get it, you know. It's fine."

"Get what?"

"We're different, you and I, just like you said." He indicated her clothes with a nod of his head. "I mean, look at you. You're perfect and put together and posh." He uncrossed his arms and gestured toward his naked chest. "And look at me. I look a mess. Tatted up and ratty and low brow."

"You're not low brow," she said. He didn't look a mess, he looked sexy and edgy, she wanted to say. But she didn't.

"I'm an artist, aren't I? A rock and roll singer. I stay up all night and sing in pubs and bars, and that doesn't fit in with whatever plan you have in that pretty head of yours. I get it."

The excitement of seeing him again, of finally talking to him, began to morph into something darker. A sickening feeling rolled in her stomach. This wasn't the reception she had anticipated.

"And no matter what I do, there are always going to be drunk fans around, and women like Emery somewhere backstage. Not that they hold a candle to you in my mind, but I can't make them disappear. And I think that's what you want."

"I know they can't disappear," she said, trying to act as if she hadn't had that very thought.

He didn't believe her, she could see it in his eyes. His expression softened and he sighed. "I guess your Professor Shipley was wrong. Not every problem has a solution."

It took a moment for his words to sink in. She gave him a quizzical look. "You talked with Professor Shipley?"

"Yes, at the ball after you left. He's an interesting man." He read the look on her face and asked, "Why?"

"I–I–I'm uncomfortable with that."

"Uncomfortable? Why?"

"I'm not sure, but knowing that you spoke with him makes me feel strange."

"Why? I'm a musician, not a leper." He sounded defensive.

"Of course you're not a leper," she said. But she didn't feel any better. "The thought of it just makes me...uncomfortable." She shrugged and something about that gesture infuriated him.

He stood up and started pacing back and forth. He stopped suddenly and said, "Do you know what you do? You compartmentalize. That's what you do." He used his hands to mime little boxes as he spoke. "There's work here, friends here, math here, art here, academics here, fun here, and none of them are allowed to touch each other." Ian made a sweeping gesture with his hands, as if knocking all of the imaginary boxes off of a table. "Well, I have news for you. Life is about touching. It's about seeing all the parts of yourself and all the parts of other people and mashing them up together into one glorious..." he looked for a word and found one, "Soup. The soup of life."

She cracked a smile, "The glorious soup of life?"

"You know what I'm getting at. Everything's not black and white. There's more to you than your work. And there's more to me than mine."

Tears pressed at the back of her eyes and she wanted to reach out to him. She wanted him to reach out to her. But neither of them did. They stood there, staring each other down, an ocean of silence between them. She tried to think of what she could say to bring the conversation back to what she had intended it to be from the beginning.

"I wanted to call you after we danced, Ian, but I couldn't think of the right words."

He looked at her, void of anger and frustration, but full of something worse. Pain.

In a voice gruff from both singing and emotion, he said, "That's the problem, Sofia. It's not about finding the exact right words or doing the exact right thing. It's not about reason and logic...it's love."

He stopped speaking, but the way he continued to look at her–into her–said more than he could have spoken with words.

Her heart was in her throat. He loved her? She tried to form a coherent response. Then, without warning, Ian ripped his eyes from hers and pushed past her, out the door.

Chapter Twenty-Eight

S ofia looked down onto the street in front of her flat through her living room window. Rain hit the glass and snaked down its smooth surface, blurring her view. With listless eyes, she stared at the spot where the lights of Luna's cab had disappeared into the grey, depressing morning.

She had walked her cousin downstairs with her suitcases just minutes before and put her in the cab that would take her back to the airport. Back to the United States.

"No, you stay home and rest," Luna had insisted when Sofia offered to ride with her and see her off properly. "You need rest." Luna had placed her small, cool hand on Sofia's cheek and Sofia had smiled softly. But no kindness could mend Sofia's heart, she knew that, and Luna knew it, too.

Sofia leaned her forehead against the cold glass of the window. A dim reflection of her eyes looked back at her, red and puffy from crying all night. Luna was gone. Everyone was gone, leaving their respective hotels and flying back home. Everyone except her.

Fat tears swelled and dropped from her eyes. She closed them. Could there really be any more tears inside of her? She thought she'd cried them all out into her pillow. Sofia groaned and pulled away from the window, going to the tissue box on her kitchen counter to blow her nose. Her nose was just as puffy and red as her eyes. It hurt when she blew it. Her head hurt, too. Throbbed.

She poured a cup of the coffee Luna had made before she left and used it to swallow some ibuprofen. She may be able to get rid of her headache, but she couldn't get the images of last night out of her mind. Ian's face. His words. They revisited her mind and cut into her heart each and every moment, pressing her down and down until she thought she would disappear into darkness.

When she'd returned to the art gallery she hadn't been capable of explaining exactly what had happened to her friends. She still couldn't. All she knew was that her world had turned dark and cold.

Sofia looked around at her empty flat, finding no comfort in it. She picked up her cell phone, its glowing screen an affront to her tired senses. No messages. No texts. She took a deep breath and blew it out through pursed lips, building up energy for what she was going to do next. Searching through her list of contacts, Sofia found what she was looking for and hit the button to call. After a few rings, the voicemail message began to play.

"Hello, you have reached Dr. Clara Weston..."

Sofia listened to the end and left her own message as directed after the beep. When she was done, she turned her phone off and left it on the counter. Shuffling into the still dark bedroom as the rain picked up outside, Sofia sank back into her bed and pulled the covers up over her head. The world outside would have to wait.

~

Sofia had never taken a sick day in her entire adult life. Let alone two in a row.

Her dark mood was impenetrable and she had not had a choice. Taking two days off to try and overcome the whole debacle of a relationship with Ian was all she could think of to do. She focused on extreme self-care and reflection. She ate chocolate and ice cream, took long baths, lit candles, slept, and slept some more. Her Mom called, Tawnyetta called, Luna and the rest of them called when they got back to Denver. She was fully supported, loved, and cared for in every way possible.

Still, her heart remained crushed and her dreary outlook on the future persisted.

She couldn't fit Ian into her life. That was clear. And his final words of love to her, which she would have thought would bring tremendous joy, instead settled in like a thick tar covering her soul. Not letting her breathe.

Ian was right. She did compartmentalize everything. She always had. And she always would. Her logical brain, her love of reason, was not conducive to falling in love. Especially falling in love with an artist like him.

Sofia stared at her reflection in her bathroom mirror. Dressing for work, because there was no way she would allow herself three sick days in a row, she had decided to embrace the fact that she and Ian were never going to happen, and she was probably going to remain alone forever.

No contacts since her eyes were still tender from crying. No makeup either, her black rimmed glasses would help mask her eyes from the world. She pulled her hair up into a high pony tail like the kind she wore when she was going to the gym and smoothed the plain white business shirt she'd pulled out of the back of her closet. Paired with simple black slacks and her low-heeled black boots, she looked as much the part of a spinster as she felt.

"Time to move on," she said to herself in the mirror.

Flicking off the bathroom light, Sofia grabbed her jacket and left for work.

The sun was not quite up yet. She had decided to head in very early and try to catch up on whatever she'd missed the past few days. The rain had finally stopped the night before and everything was wet and chilly as she walked toward the Thames. She pulled her jacket tighter. The humidity in the air made the bite of the cold fall morning even sharper.

She heard the first notes as she walked through the quiet hall that led to her office door. They floated to her ear so softly, she almost thought she was hearing things. An almost empty university at the break of dawn was not the place she expected to hear...was it jazz music? As Sofia got closer to her office door, the sound grew louder, and she recognized the fluid and sultry tone of a saxophone. Once at the door, she knew the music was coming from inside. It stopped and started again, not like a recorded song, but rather like someone practicing playing a song.

Sofia pushed the door open slowly, not sure if she was supposed to witness whatever was happening inside. To her surprise she found Professor Shipley perched on the edge of the conference table, his eyes closed, playing the saxophone.

She looked around. Nobody else was there. The music stopped and Professor Shipley opened his eyes, looking at her with some surprise.

"Dr. Venegas," he said.

"I'm sorry," Sofia said uncertainly. "I didn't mean to interrupt."

Professor Shipley lowered the saxophone and let it rest against his thigh. "Nonsense," he said brusquely, waving her in, "this is a work area." She stepped in, but felt awkward, as if she didn't actually have a job there. He eyed her over his glasses, "We weren't sure you were going to make it in today. Sick, were you?"

Sofia nodded, trying to look sincere. She wasn't really lying. She had been too sick to come in. Lovesick counted as sick, didn't it?

"You look tired. Are you sure you're not still sick?" His large eyes widened even larger, apparently alarmed at the idea she might be spreading germs.

"No, I'm much better now," she reassured him. "I'm just a little sleepy from getting up earlier than normal."

"Yes," he peered at her again. "You're here quite early."

"I thought I would make up some work since I've been gone. I didn't know you would be here..." Sofia's eyes fell to the saxophone. She wasn't sure what to say about it.

"Oh, this," Professor Shipley chuckled quietly as he regarded the instrument in his hand. Sofia watched this uncommon show of good humor with curiosity. "I practice every morning. Though by the sound of it you may not be able to tell." He smiled at her, and again she was perplexed at his friendliness. "It helps, you know. Music doesn't just help the soul...it helps the mind." He emphasized his point by tapping one finger against his temple.

Sofia mumbled her agreement. A pang of regret shot through her body. She didn't want to talk about music right now.

"Do you play any instruments?" Professor Shipley inquired.

"No, I don't."

He grunted. "You listen to music, though?"

"Yes, of course." She was having a hard time disguising her discomfort on the topic.

Professor Shipley observed her for a few beats before turning his attention back to the saxophone. "You wouldn't think the two were related. Music and math. Unless you choose to look deeper." He stood and began putting the saxophone away in a case that lay open on the table behind him.

"In reality they are deeply entwined. They just appear different on the surface. Do you agree, Dr. Venegas?"

Sofia was taken aback. Though she couldn't be sure Professor Shipley was trying to tell her anything in particular, his words were eerily on point. His gaze sharpened as he looked at her awaiting an answer.

"Yes, I agree," she answered quickly.

"That's the way life is, sometimes, Dr. Venegas. Take Clara and I, for example."

"Dr. Clara?"

He nodded and clicked the saxophone case shut. He held his right hand out, palm up. "She is a babbling, excitable, unconventional and, let's be honest, quite peculiar old girl." He looked at her and Sofia had no choice but to silently concur. Then he held up his left hand, palm up. "And I am a blustering, mean spirited, stubborn old codger." He raised his bushy eyebrows at Sofia, daring her to disagree. She did not. "And yet..." he clasped his two hands together as if he was greeting himself with a warm handshake, "Together we make an excellent team."

Before she could stop it, a laugh escaped her lips. But when Professor Shipley eyed her, she could see amusement in his look. He was trying to entertain her. A tiny warmth flared in the center of her stomach and for the first time since she'd started working there, Sofia felt like she belonged.

Something else began to stir inside of her. An idea. A feeling that had come loose and was releasing into her system. The sensation flooded her veins and was overtaking her entire body so quickly, she felt a little lightheaded.

"Professor Shipley?" she asked.

"Yes?"

"Would you mind if I took another day off?"

Chapter Twenty-Nine

She had to call Tawnyetta for directions.

"Yes, I have it. I'll text it to you," Tawnyetta told her after listening to Sofia's rushed request for Ian's home address. There was a moment's pause where neither of them said anything, then Tawnyetta exclaimed, "This is so exciting! How romantic."

Sofia laughed out loud. Even though she was out of breath from hurrying down the street on foot, determined to get to Ian's flat as quickly as she could, the thrill of knowing she was on her way to see him was all powerful.

"We'll see how it works out," she cautioned, but she had an uncharacteristically positive feeling about her decision to find Ian and...and...she wasn't sure yet. She just needed to see him. To talk to him. A text or phone call seemed too trite given their last conversation. Whatever she was going to do had to be done in person. She would figure out the rest when she got there.

Tawnyetta texted the address and Sofia saw she was less than a ten-minute walk away. However, it did not take her anywhere near ten minutes and she did not walk. She flew.

When she reached up and knocked on the door to his flat, her hand was steady and sure. For a long moment she worried he wasn't there and she would be left dead in the water. Then she heard the lock click and she thought her heart might burst out of her chest it was beating so hard. The door pulled open and Sofia's heart sank.

"Good Lord," Emery said, looking Sofia up and down. "You're buggering about again?"

Sofia's enthusiasm was dimmed, but not extinguished. She remembered what Ian had told her about there always being an Emery around. Focusing on the part when he had said none of them held a candle to her, Sofia cleared her throat and said, "Is Ian here?"

Hugh, the bass player, popped his head around the corner of the door. "Oh, hello," he said kindly.

"Hi," Sofia said, grateful for his friendly smile. Emery rolled her eyes and yanked the door open all the way, indicating Sofia could come in if she wanted to, but it might ruin Emery's day. "I need to speak to Ian," Sofia reiterated, not moving inside.

"He's not here," Emery called out over her shoulder.

Sofia could see most of the living room with the door wide open. In addition to Hugh and Emery, the other guitarist and the drummer were there, Danny and Charlie. No Ian.

Hugh gave Sofia an apologetic look, "He's not here, sorry." He indicated with a sweep of his arm that she should enter. "You can wait here if you like." There was an awkward pause as all of the band members waited for her to step inside the flat. Emery snorted her disapproval.

Sofia thanked them for their offer, but didn't stay. She knew that she needed to see Ian in private. Their reunion would have to wait, though waiting was excruciating.

She was halfway down the block from his flat when she

heard, "Oi!" Turning at the sound, Sofia saw Hugh jogging in her direction. She waited for him.

When he reached her, he was a bit out of breath, and appeared a little out of sorts. "Look...I know Ian would want to talk to you. Are you sure you won't wait?"

"Thank you for saying that, but..." Sofia glanced at the building they had just come from. "I don't think so." She looked back at Hugh. "You don't know where he went?"

"No, we were rehearsing. Then Emery showed up with some invitation for the band to go on a morning show and Ian, well, he just took off. He's been a little off lately." Hugh gave her a meaningful look and Sofia's soul lifted. In his band member buddy way, he was trying to tell her that Ian missed her.

She smiled at him and asked, "He just left without saying anything?"

"All he said is he needed to clear his head. That doesn't help much, I know."

Sofia's stomach did a flip-flop and her smile slowly widened. "Actually, Hugh, it helps a lot."

By the time she got to The London Eye the day had dawned and a warming sun shone down through puffy white clouds. No more dreary grey clouds. She smiled at the sun as she made her way to the gigantic Ferris wheel contraption. The weather mirrored her growing sense of optimism.

There were throngs of people in the area. All of them enjoying the morning as much as she was, though she imagined none of them could possibly be on the same quest. She was here to find the man she loved and tell him how she felt. It seemed impossibly dramatic, but that was the truth. He had been right about her trying to keep everything separate and never trusting that even though they were very different from one another, they were actually a perfect match. She needed to tell him that he had been right and that she wanted to be with him.

She scanned the crowded line leading up to the bottom of The London Eye where groups loaded onto the pod, were shut in by automatic doors and lifted more than 400 feet into the air. She didn't see him anywhere amongst the families and tourists and for a brief moment she thought perhaps she had been wrong. Perhaps he hadn't come here to look out over the city and clear his head.

Then she saw him.

He was unmistakable, even from behind, with his deep red hair, lean frame, and worn leather jacket. He was at the very front of the line, grouped with the next set of people ready to board the empty pod heading their way. There was no way she could reach him by running through the line.

"Ian!" she shouted, drawing the attention of people in her immediate area, but not him. Ignoring the looks, she shouted again, this time waving her arms in the air, "Ian!"

The empty pod was in front of him now and the group he was with began to board. An elderly man next to him said something to Ian and she saw his profile as he responded and they chatted for a moment. Ian gestured for the elderly man to get on the pod in front of him. In a moment he would be boarded and on the pod and lifted into the air without her, and even though it wasn't logical to be anxious about that fact, Sofia was overwhelmed with urgency.

"Ian, wait!" This time she waved her arms and jumped up and down. Even though the crowd around her was giving her a wide birth, probably concerned she had lost her marbles, she continued shouting and jumping as Ian stepped onto the pod.

Then a miracle. He heard her. Or at least she thought he did. He turned sharply in her direction, a quizzical expression on his face. Sofia's heart leapt in her chest at the sight of his beautiful face.

"Ian! Ian!" She jumped higher and waved harder until the activity caught his attention and they locked eyes. "Wait!" she shouted again.

A moment hung between them. A singular moment in time where absolutely everything else, the people, the street, the giant London Eye, the earth itself, ceased to exist. The confusion on his face fell away and he stared at her like she was a vision, a dream that had come true.

"Ian..." Sofia almost whispered. No longer waving and jumping she stood locked in his gaze, waiting for him to react. Then, it happened. His face broke into the widest smile she'd ever seen him smile. A brilliant beaming welcoming smile that was immediately covered by the closing of the pod doors.

Realizing what was happening, Ian lunged forward, but not soon enough. The glass doors were firmly shut and the pod gently lifted him away from her into the air. He hit the glass with his palm and she could see his mouth forming her name, "Sofia!"

As she watched him look around in vain for some way to stop the pod she felt a surge of love so strong that tears started streaming down her face even as she laughed out loud at the absurdity of it all. She covered her mouth with her hand as he moved higher and higher until she couldn't see into his pod any longer.

Struck with a new idea, she reached into her purse and grabbed her phone. Her fingers were trembling so hard and her vision was so blurred with joyful tears, it took a few moments before she found his number and punched the button. Before it even rang once he answered.

"Sofia," he said. Hearing his voice say her name brought a new flow of tears.

"Ian..."

"What's wrong? Are you all right?" He could hear her crying.

"I'm fine, I'm fine," she got herself under control.

"Thank God," he muttered.

"I came to find you."

"You did?"

Her heart was racing and her hands had turned to ice, but she had to tell him, she had to say the words. "I need to tell you something."

He paused. "Okay."

"I was wrong, Ian. I don't want us to just be friends."

He paused again, letting her words sink in. "You don't?"

She shook her head as if he could see her. Then she took a shuddering breath and said, "No, I don't–because–because– I'm in love with you."

Another pause, and for a split second Sofia was more terrified than she'd ever been, wondering what he was going to say. When he spoke, his voice was low and full of disbelief. "*You're* in love with *me*?" he asked.

"Yes," she said, waited, then again to be sure he understood, "I'm in love with you, Ian." She looked up at the pods, wishing she could see his face.

He made a sound that was a mixture of a laugh and a cough. After a few beats he continued, louder than before and clear as a bell, maybe to make sure she understood as well, "I'm in love with you, too, Sofia." The words rushed around her like a warm wind and she wanted nothing more than to be in his arms.

Voices rose on the other end of the call, apparently talking to Ian. He spoke a muffled, "She loves me." Shouts of happy encouragement rose up around him and Sofia realized he'd told the entire pod of people. She laughed out loud.

"Where are you, Luv?" he said into the phone. She waved upwards so he could see her better even though she didn't know where he was. "Oh, there you are, I can see you," he said. "God, you're beautiful."

She was laughing and crying and generally making a scene on the ground. "I'm sorry I've been so confused. I didn't know what to do. I still don't know how everything is going to work."

"It's going to be brilliant. We're going to be brilliant. Don't you worry about it," he said. There was another pause and he said, "I do know one thing for absolute certain."

"What's that?"

"This is going to be the longest 30 minutes of my bloody life."

When he finally stepped off the slow moving pod he was followed by a group of tourists who were slapping his back and offering heartfelt encouragement, but Ian only had eyes for her. Instead of following the exit ramp, he hopped over the iron bars so he could get to her faster. They rushed into each other's arms and he lifted her up off the ground in a bear hug so tight she could hardly breathe. Sofia didn't care. She was safe in his arms and she would never push him away again.

"I love you," he said into her neck as he held her close.

Sofia wrapped her arms tighter around his neck, wanting him to hold her like this forever. "I love you, too," she whispered.

He put her down gently on the ground and lifted one hand to cup her chin, which she tilted up toward him.

The scent of his cologne mixed with the smell of leather from his coat and drove her crazy with desire. As he searched her face, taking in every bit of her and loving all of it, she placed her palm on his cheek, letting her fingers trace down his beard and along the tattoo on his neck.

They gazed at each other, anticipating this kiss with their whole hearts. And when their lips finally touched something fused inside of both of them, like stars melting together, making their souls one.

Nothing else after that moment could ever make her think

he wasn't the perfect man for her. Sofia knew without a doubt there was nobody else in the world who could ever hold a candle to her Ian.

The End

A whirlwind enveloped Sofia and Ian as soon as they became a couple.

Ian and the band released a new CD, which promptly shot to the top of the charts, first in the UK, then in the US. The Robot Tellers changed their name to The Tellers, as Ian explained, "...everybody calls us The Tellers anyway. Why fight it?" And the years and years of work he had put into being a performer finally paid off.

Not only that, but shortly after her first Christmas in London, their first together, Sofia was offered an assistant professorship at King's College, which meant more work, but also more prestige and more money.

Still, throughout it all, their relationship only grew stronger. Sofia was continually reminded how correct Professor Shipley had been when he said that math and music complemented each other. Whenever the travel and performing and general chaos of the life of a rock star got to be too much for Ian, he could sink into the relative calm and predictable life Sofia led with her students and classes at the University. He would often bring dinner by her office when she was working late or come to her flat so they could relax, stay in and watch a movie together.

As far as Sofia went, whenever the steady and reliable life she had built in London became a little boring, she had Ian to turn to, and his wild and exciting rock and roll lifestyle never failed to provide an adequate distraction. Either she would join him and the band at rehearsals or go out on the town after a concert, or she would travel with him over the weekend to Berlin or Prague or other exciting European cities she had never seen. There he would perform, which was always a treat, and they would explore the city together the next day. Their life as boyfriend and girlfriend was like one long dream date that neither of them wanted to end.

"I have a question," Sofia said. They were curled up on her couch together, their hands entwined. Instead of watching the movie they had selected for the night, Sofia was tracing his Let it Be tattoo with the tip of her finger.

"What is it, Luv?" He kissed her temple after he said it, a habit Sofia adored.

"Are you ever going to get a tattoo for me?" She turned in his arms to look at him with a coy smile.

"Oh, ho ho," he chuckled. He gave her his best flirtatious look, which turned her heart into goo every single time. He tapped his finger over his heart, saying with a wink, "Right here. I'm saving a space for you."

It wasn't long after that conversation that Ian appeared at her office in the middle of the day, something he rarely did without calling or texting first. He was anxious, agitated, and Sofia had a momentary concern that something terrible was wrong. It turned out to be the complete opposite.

"They want me in Los Angeles by May 25th," he explained. He had just finished telling her about not one, but two new developments. First, he had been asked to write music for a film being made in California. It was supposedly a

Pirates of the Caribbean meets Rocky Horror Picture Show and Ian would be the composer. They wanted him to start writing the music right away and be on set over the summer. The second thing was even bigger. The Tellers had been offered a deal with a major record label that wanted to release their CD's and send them on a world tour.

"That's fantastic!" Sofia told him.

"It is, isn't it?" He was excited, she could see that much. But something was bothering him.

"What's the matter?"

He looked at her, deep concern in his beautiful golden eyes. "I don't want all of this to mess us up," he confessed. "I know how you need to plan and be stable, and I'm not sure how all of this will work out."

That's where she stopped him. "Ian Law," she said in her most scolding tone. "If you've taught me anything, you've taught me that I can do with a little adventure in my life." His face started to relax and the happiness she saw in his eyes made her want to encourage him more. "This is your dream! My God, this is amazing!"

"So you're okay with this? Big changes are ahead," he said.

Sofia put her palm on his cheek, smiling up at him, so certain of their love that no life adventure would ever frighten her again. "No matter what, we will be brilliant," she said.

He flashed her his most shining smile yet and answered, "Yes...we will be brilliant."

And they were.

Angie...

A breeze swept off the ocean and through Angie's red, curly locks, pulling them back from her face and lifting them in wisps that floated lightly behind her head. The breeze was cool and damp and brushed her cheeks tenderly. It refreshed her and filled her with a deep sense of relief that would be difficult to explain to another soul. Not that anyone was asking.

Angie turned to look at Sofia who had left the water's edge and hiked back to the parking lot at the top of beach, looking for better cell reception. She stood neatly next to their rented convertible carefully removing each of her high heel sandals and dumping the sand out of them, all while speaking efficiently into her cell phone. Probably to her realtor.

The breeze picked up, sending Angie's deep red hair tumbling across her eyes and mouth as if the Pacific Ocean was protesting her lack of attention. She turned back, heeding the water's call. She would follow the whims of the tide, it was her way. The ocean, after all, was why she was here. Why she had agreed to come to California.

Of course, she had been happy to join Sofia and Ian on their house hunt in Los Angeles. They were in need of a rental since they would be spending most of the summer in California. With Ian wrapped up in his music work, Sofia was in want of a house hunting buddy. Angie welcomed the chance to get away from her job at the metaphysical bookstore, which had soured lately into an overly commercialized and draining existence. Plus it was a wonderful opportunity to spend a week with one of her dearest friends.

That being said, it was the call of the open water that had added the extra push Angie needed to come all the way from Colorado. It had been ages since she'd been near an ocean, or at least it seemed like ages.

"Are you ready to go?" Sofia's voice called to her, thinned by the space between them and the persistent wind.

Angie sighed. She wasn't ready to leave just yet. She could stay on the beach all day without ever tiring of its strength and magical beauty. The sound of the waves, the fresh scent of water and salt in the air, the sunshine.

Still, duty called.

Angie turned and waved agreeably to Sofia. "I'm coming," she called out, though she was fairly certain the ocean stole her words and whisked them away across the water.

She made her way up the slight slope of the beach, her leather flip-flops dangling from her hand. Her toes squished into the sand as she walked, warming them deliciously, and giving her a good workout to boot.

As she neared their white convertible another car, a black sports car, approached slowly and parked next to Sofia. Where their rental was cute and round and looked like it belonged driving alongside the waterfront, this car was shining and sleek. Its slick lines and gleaming chrome screamed 'money', even to someone like Angie, who lacked any knowledge of expensive sports cars.

"Hullo, ladies," Ian exclaimed as he unfolded from the passenger side of the black car.

"Hi, darling," Sofia beamed at him. Sofia was always beaming at Ian. Adorable.

"Hi," Angie called out to him as she took advantage of the foot shower located at the edge of the parking lot to wash the sand from her bare feet and put her shoes back on.

Ian waved happily back to her and went to Sofia's side, kissing her warmly on the cheek. Another man, a stranger to Angie, rose from the driver's seat. Tall, dark, and immaculate, very much like his car, there was something vaguely familiar about him. Angie couldn't put her finger on what.

Though she had only been in L.A. for a few days, Angie had noticed the high ratio of extremely attractive people in the population. She and Sofia had discussed it, in fact, and put it down to the fact that more people were here to break into show business and they had to work regular jobs to survive. Waiters and waitresses, bus drivers and police, store clerks and even the people at the car rental place at the airport, were more likely to be drop dead gorgeous than anywhere else Angie had ever been. Los Angeles was literally bursting with pretty people. Even though she'd been inundated with beauty the past few days, as Ian's friend turned in her direction, Angie was astonished at the sight of him.

His white short sleeved pullover showed off deep brown skin and well formed muscles. His firm jawline, strong, slightly thin nose, and midnight black hair rippling in perfect waves added up to an incredibly striking appearance. But it was his dazzling brown eyes, which twinkled at her as he removed expensive sunglasses, that truly did her in. As she struggled to overcome the shock she was experiencing from merely looking at him, she had the epiphany that black sports car man was the most magnificent man she had ever seen.

"Hello," he said. His voice held her in rapt attention, yet she was still too stunned to speak. Not just because of his incredible looks. It was his voice. Deep and soothing, intensely masculine...and...familiar. She knew that voice.

Angie glanced at Sofia and saw that she, too, was a little taken aback at the sight of this glamorous man and his glamorous car, with the voice that brought back memories. Angie was reminded of something from their teenage years. A TV show. That's where she had heard his voice. Angie looked back at the man who was smiling at them, his teeth brilliantly white against rich dark skin.

Ian began the introduction, "Allow me to introduce–"

"Peter Pineapple!" Angie blurted out. The name of the cartoon show had come back to her suddenly, not allowing for any filters.

Peter Pineapple's smile faltered.

It was Ian's turn to look stunned, then confused. "Sorry?"

Sofia gave Angie a nod of agreement before turning tactfully to the tall, dark stranger and asking, "Did you play Peter in Peter Pineapple?"

With a stiff smile he confirmed their suspicions. "I was the voice of Peter, yes."

There was a long pause where Peter Pineapple didn't seem to know what else to say, and neither did Sofia. Ian appeared to be clueless about the popular American cartoon show. And Angie...Angie was still held captive by the sight of Peter Pineapple, who was probably perfect. She was also having a hard time reconciling the amazing looking man in front of her with the fat, yellow cartoon character she had loved in high school.

Peter Pineapple cleared his throat and, in an effort to smooth over the awkwardness that hung in the air, introduced himself, "My name is Xavier Patel."

Full recognition now flooded over Sofia who nodded enthusiastically as she said, "Yes, of course. I've seen you in several movies."

Xavier smiled stiffly at her, his good looks unable to hide some discomfort that lingered just under the surface of his expression. He ducked his head and put his sunglasses back on before answering, "Yes, perhaps."

"Xave is starring in the pirate movie," Ian explained, pronouncing the shortening of Xavier as 'ha-vee'. The pirate movie was the movie Ian was scoring over the summer, one of the reasons he and Sofia were in L.A. "Xave, this is Sofia," Ian introduced his girlfriend with pride.

Xave nodded at Sofia in greeting. Then, turning his shaded eyes to Angie who remained hovering on the edge of the parking lot, droplets of water still running off of her feet, he asked, "And what is your name?"

Angie wasn't sure he really wanted to know. She couldn't tell without seeing the expression in his eyes and there was an austere politeness in his tone that gave her the feeling he didn't want to be here talking to them at all. His aura had dimmed after she mentioned Peter Pineapple. She still felt flustered. It wasn't like her to respond so strongly to someone's surface appearance. She wasn't usually this shallow.

"Angie," she answered. And for some unexplained reason she continued with, "Short for Angela."

Xave's lips twitched, but did not smile. He continued to look at her for a long moment, his eyes hidden by the sunglasses. Angie's pulse quickened in response. The whole vibe was puzzling. Was she attracted to him? Insulted? Afraid? She couldn't tell.

"An angel in our midst," Xave said, his deep voice floating through the air and touching her skin ever so lightly. Angie shivered, though the day was warm and the sun was shining.

Just then a heavy gust of wind came off the ocean and blew across them, flapping their clothes and tangling Angie's long hair across her face.

An omen. A sign that this was a significant moment in her life, or a warning, Angie didn't know which.

The End

Do you want to know how Angie's dreams come true? Find out in *Her Sheltered Cove*

Also by Darci Balogh

<u>Dream Come True Sweet Romance</u>

1. Her Scottish Keep

2. Her British Bard

3. Her Sheltered Cove

<u>The Mighty Aphrodite Writing Society</u>

1. Beach Retreat at Turtle Cove

2. Beach Wedding at Turtle Cove

<u>Lady Billionaire Series</u>

1. Ms. Money Bags

2. Ms. Perfect

<u>Sweet Holiday Romance Series</u>

Holiday romances for Halloween through New Year's Eve!

1. Enchanting Eve

2. Love is at the Table

3. Mistletoe Madness

4. New Year in Paradise

<u>Sugar Plum Romance Series</u>

Christmas, cooking, and chefs falling in love!

1. Charlotte's Christmas Charade

2. Bella's Christmas Blunder

~

About the Author

Darci Balogh is a writer and indie filmmaker from Denver. She grew up in the beautiful mountains of Colorado and has lived in several areas of the state over her lifetime. She currently resides in Denver where she raised her two glorious, intelligent daughters to functioning adulthood. This is, by far, one of her highest achievements.

Darci has a love-hate relationship with gardening, probably should dust more, adores dogs and is allergic to cats. She has been a writer since she was a child and enjoys crafting stories into novels and screenplays. Big surprise, some of her favorite pastimes are reading and watching movies. Classic British TV is high on her 'Like' list, along with quietly depressing detective series and coffee with heavy cream.

For more romance books by Darci Balogh, click through to the Also by page or visit www.knowheremedia.com/books

www.ingramcontent.com/pod-product-compliance
Lightning Source LLC
Chambersburg PA
CBHW050843190726

48286CB00007B/2205